KU-755-215

# A GOOD HIDING

## and other stories

### Written and illustrated by
### WIM HOFMAN

Translated from the Dutch by
LANCE SALWAY

CLASS NO J823·08 HOF
ITEM NO 3300239843
THE LIBRARY
WESTMINSTER COLLEGE
OXFORD OX2 9AT

TURTON & CHAMBERS

© 1989 Unieboek b.v., the Netherlands
English translation © 1991 Lance Salway
First published in the Netherlands
under the title *Straf en andere verhalen*
by Van Holkema & Warendorf

First published in England and Australia 1991

No part of this publication may be reproduced,
stored in a retrieval system, or transmitted
in any form, or by any means, electronic,
mechanical, photocopying, recording,
or otherwise, without the prior permission
of the copyright holder

Turton & Chambers Ltd
Station Road, Woodchester
Stroud, Glos GL5 5EQ, England
and 10 Armagh Street
Victoria Park, Perth
Western Australia 6100

Typesetting by
Alan Sutton, Stroud
Printed in England by
Short Run Press, Exeter

Catalogue–in–Publication Data
available from the British Library

ISBN 1 872148 40 9

# CONTENTS

# A good hiding

Elsie is sitting at the table in the kitchen. She must stay there until she has eaten up all her supper and it is nowhere near finished yet. In front of her there is a plate with a helping of rice, a helping of curry sauce, a helping of peas and some pieces of meat. One of the pieces of meat looks different from the others. It is lighter in colour and a bit tattered. It has already been chewed. But Elsie couldn't get it down her throat. The more she chewed, the more tattered it became.

'I really don't like it,' she'd said.

'Of course you do,' was her father's answer. 'Come on now, eat it up. This time you're really going to eat it. Every evening it's the same old story: I don't like it, I don't like it . . . But now you're going to eat it all up and I don't want to see a single crumb left on your plate. Understand?'

But when she didn't eat it she got a smack round the ear. And her mother said that she could easily finish it in a couple of mouthfuls.

But she couldn't do it. And that's why she has been

sitting for ages in the kitchen, staring at the plate and sobbing.

The rice is cold and sticky and congealed, the curry sauce looks like green slime and she knows that if she tries to prick the peas with her fork they'll jump right off the plate. But the meat is the nastiest of all. It makes her shudder just to look at it. And so she doesn't eat.

Outside the sun sinks behind the houses and the sky quickly changes colour. Children are still playing in the alleyway between the sheds. Hide-and-seek, by the sound of it. Elsie would like to go out and play too. She knows some really good hiding places.

Now her father has come into the kitchen to make some coffee. He rinses the coffee pot, fills the kettle, tears open a packet of ground coffee.

'You're not getting very far with that,' he says then.

Elsie sobs. 'I really don't like it.'

'You're going to eat it up just the same,' her father says. He lights the gas with a lighter in the shape of a pistol. 'You're going to eat it all up. Even if you have to sit there till midnight. This time you're going to clear your plate, understand? You needn't think you're in charge here. Come on now, put a piece of meat in your mouth!'

Elsie shakes her head.

'Are you telling me that you won't? Well, we'll soon see about that.'

Father puts the coffee pot down very carefully, as if he is trying to glue the thing to the table. Then he picks up the fork and jabs it into a lump of meat. The

8

fork squeaks across the bottom of the plate. Then he dangles the piece of meat in front of Elsie's mouth as if the fork is a hook with bait on it and Elsie the fish who must bite it.

But the fish doesn't bite. Elsie keeps her mouth tightly closed, biting her lower lip. She is angry and frightened and so she closes her eyes as well.

'Open up!' Father shouts. 'Or do you want me to force it in?'

Elsie is crying now with her mouth closed. A bubble of snot comes out of her nose.

Father pushes the meat against her lips and so she has to take it.

'Now chew it!' Father shouts.

But Elsie doesn't chew it. Instead she spits the meat out at once and it lands in the sink.

'Right, that's the last straw!' her father shouts. 'Have you gone crazy or something? What on earth do you think you're playing at?' He gives her such a hard slap that she bumps her head against the cupboard.

'Get upstairs, you!' Father yells. 'And be quick about it!'

She stumbles into the hall.

'Get up to bed. Hurry up now, and don't let me hear another peep out of you. I'm sick to death of you!'

Elsie crawls quickly up the stairs on her hands and knees and slips into bed with all her clothes on. She is crying so much that the bed is shaking but she tries to do it as quietly as she can.

Can she help it if she doesn't like the food? Mind

you, there isn't much that she does like to eat. She doesn't like omelettes or endives or parsley or curry and rice or onions or leeks or chicory or mushrooms or stew . . . Every day there is always something that she doesn't like. And the more things that she doesn't like the more often she gets a good hiding . . . It would be best if Elsie never ate anything ever again. Then she wouldn't have to sit at the table any more and her parents wouldn't need to hit her again either.

It is grey in her room now. On one of the walls there is a streak of light. This comes from the street lamp that stands in front of the house. Every now and then a car drives past. There is even more light in the little room then. Someone is whistling outside and she can hear a dog barking. There are damp patches on her pillow and her handkerchief is wet through. It is a long time before she falls asleep.


When Elsie comes downstairs the next morning, her father and mother are very quiet. They are sitting at the breakfast table. Father is reading the paper and Mother is smoking a cigarette.

Last night's plate is pushed in front of her.

'And eat it all up!' Father says.

Elsie looks at the food. The curry sauce has turned dark green and the peas are wrinkled. The chunks of meat look just as horrible as before.

Elsie says nothing. She stares at the mess on her plate and shudders. She feels tears welling up once more, but something else is welling up too: a black cloud of anger and disgust. She picks up the plate

10

very slowly and throws the whole lot on the floor by her chair.

Father and Mother start to shout like anything. They rush towards her and her face is slapped so hard that blood trickles from her nose and her lip.

'Are you crazy or what?' Father shouts. 'You're still going to eat it all.' And he pushes her on to the floor.

'I don't like it. I don't like it. I don't like it . . .' Elsie whimpers.

'Leave her alone,' says Mother. 'Or else there'll be another accident. I don't think she wants any food at

all. I don't think she wants to live here any more. If she wants to leave then we mustn't stand in her way. She'd better just pack her suitcase and clear out. We don't need an awful child like her . . .'

The upshot of it all is that Father and Mother go angrily off to work, leaving Elsie to clear up the mess before she can go to school. The rice and the peas are gobbled up by the vacuum cleaner. It always eats everything.

'You're awfully late, child,' says the teacher at school. 'Did you have a fall? Your lip's very swollen. Go and sit down and take out your arithmetic book. Start right away. We've reached exercise thirty-four.'

Exercise thirty-four consists of columns of adding up. The sums aren't really difficult but Elsie can't settle down to them. She picks at her sore nose for a bit and gets blood on her finger and on her exercise book too and her handkerchief is very dirty. But what really worries her is the question: What shall I take with me? She has a little suitcase at home that will fit perfectly on the carrier of her bicycle and it holds a good deal. She must take a jersey, some pyjamas, her money-box, a toothbrush . . .

When school is over she goes home right away to look for her things and to pack the suitcase. She puts some clothes inside it, and her toothbrush, a handkerchief, her money-box that looks like a dice. There are more than twenty guilders in it. Pocket money, and money that Grandma has given her, and the coin she found at the bus stop. She puts her alarm clock into the case as well. There isn't room for anything else.

Her mother is busy in the garden. She is wearing yellow gloves and pruning the roses.

'And where do you think you're going?' she asks as Elsie walks quietly down the garden path with her suitcase.

'I'm going away,' Elsie says. She walks to her bicycle which is leaning against the shed.

'What do you mean, away?' her mother asks as she clips a branch into small pieces which she throws on to a pile.

'Just away,' says Elsie. She puts the suitcase on the back of her bicycle.

'Well, just so long as you're back in time for supper,' says Mother.

'I don't want anything to eat,' says Elsie. 'I don't feel like anything.'

'Now don't start all that again!' Mother shouts.

'What's going on now?' asks Father, who has arrived home earlier than usual.

Elsie fastens the suitcase to the carrier. She quickly pushes her bike in the direction of the gate.

'Elsie's going away,' says Mother. 'She's going away on her bicycle and she won't be back for supper.'

'Well, that's marvellous, that is!' Father answers. 'In a word: brilliant! Well, just let her try it. She'll soon find out that home isn't so bad after all. Go on then! Off with you! Quick march!' He waves his hand as though he is shooing away a swarm of irritating flies.

He naturally expects her to say something or else to

change her mind and come back, but Elsie is already out of the gate and riding quickly past the houses. She looks over her shoulder and is amazed to see that her father isn't running after her.

She pedals quickly and is soon well on the way to Grandma's: a half-hour ride along a stretch of cycle track beside the main road. There are puddles here and there on the cycle track and Elsie likes to ride straight through them. Sometimes the water splashes so high that she has to lift up her legs. A piece of newspaper is floating in one of the puddles and she aims straight for the middle of it. Her father always says that it isn't wise to ride through puddles. Anything could be lying there: glass, nails and all sorts of other rubbish.

She rides past a field and some cows start to run when Elsie waves at them. She hardly notices that she is being followed by a car. She only realizes it when the car hoots and drives close beside her. She knows this car. Her parents are sitting inside it. Her mother winds down the window and shouts something. But Elsie just pedals on.

'Elsie, stop a moment!' Mother calls through the window.

Elsie barely gives her a glance.

'Stop a moment! Where on earth are you going?'

Elsie shrugs her shoulders and pedals on.

'It'll be dark soon,' says her mother. 'And it's going to rain. Can't you see those dark clouds?'

The sky is indeed full of dark blue clouds. And she can already feel drops of rain.

'Why don't you come with us instead?' pleads her

mother. She is getting annoyed by the rain and by the wind blowing her hair into a tangle. She pulls her head inside the car and talks to Father.

Then she shouts: 'Are you on your way to Grandma's, by any chance?'

Elsie nods.

'Well, stop then!' her mother shouts. 'We'll take you there. We can put your bike in the back. Come on now, stop!'

Elsie stops and her father puts the suitcase and the bicycle in the boot. The bicycle doesn't fit properly and so it sticks out a little.

No one says anything in the car. Her mother lights a cigarette, puffs out clouds of smoke and closes the window. Elsie thinks that cigarette smoke is horrible but she is glad to be sitting inside because it is raining properly now, and the windscreen wipers are swishing angrily from side to side.

There is a lot of talking when they get to Grandma's, but Elsie doesn't say anything. She watches television and sees how you can weave baskets from raffia, and is given a sandwich and a slice of gingerbread.

'There, you see? She's eating now,' says Grandma.

'Oh yes, snacks, she'll eat those,' says her mother, who is drinking tea and eating a doughnut.

After a while, when Grandma's clock strikes six, Father says: 'Come on, it's time we were on our way. Perhaps she's calmed down now. She hasn't been herself lately and we can't do anything with her.'

But when she is putting on her coat Elsie says: 'And now I'd like my bike, and my suitcase.'

15

'What do you mean?' asks Father. 'Surely you're coming home with us in the car?'

'I don't want to,' says Elsie.

'But it's still raining,' says Mother. 'Surely you're not going to ride back in the rain?'

'I'm not going back,' says Elsie.

'What do you want to do, then?' asks Grandma. 'Do you want to stay here?'

'I've had enough of this!' Father shouts. 'She's coming with us.'

He grabs Elsie firmly by the shoulder. It's just as well she's got her coat on.

'I want to stay with Grandma . . .' says Elsie.

'Oh, let her stay if she wants to,' says Grandma.

'There you are, she's getting her own way again,' says Father but, in the end, he gives in and fetches Elsie's case from the car. 'We're taking the bicycle with us,' he says. 'We'll come and collect her tomorrow morning at about eight. Then she'll be in good time for school. And perhaps she'll have come to her senses by then, too.'

'We'll have a nice look at the telly,' says Grandma when the car has at long last turned out of the street. 'And after that you can have a nice long sleep.'

And they go inside to watch the television: part of a consumer affairs programme, a story with crashing cars in it, and figure skating, in which a girl falls over a bunch of flowers that has been left on the ice. Because she has fallen over she only gets low marks.

Grandma eats a bowl of porridge while they are watching. She sprinkles sugar on it.

'I don't suppose you'd like any of this?' she asks.

'No, ugh!' says Elsie, and sticks out her tongue.

'Well, I like nothing better,' says Grandma. The porridge disappears into her mouth bit by bit. And later on Grandma fetches a bottle of sherry and a glass from the cupboard.

'I always have a glass of sherry before I go to bed,' she says.

But this time she drinks two glasses and the announcer on the television says: 'Goodnight and see you tomorrow.'

'How silly,' says Elsie. 'He can't see us, can he?'

'No,' says Grandma, 'but we can see him.'

'Not really,' says Elsie.

Grandma switches off the television.

'Anyway, we're going to bed,' she says then.

The bed in Grandma's spare room is big and smells fresh and clean. Beside it, a white earthenware elephant is standing on a little table. There is a hole in the animal's back with a cactus in it. Elsie puts her alarm clock beside the elephant and pulls a little cord to put out the light.

Grandma, who has come to wish her goodnight, sees the luminous hands of the alarm clock.

'That's a good idea,' she says. 'You must be up in good time. Your father will be at the door at about eight o'clock. Sleep well.'

The bed is a ship in which she sails into the night.

Just after six the alarm goes off and wakes Elsie. She gets up and creeps cautiously out of her room with her suitcase in one hand and her shoes in the other. But even though she tries to walk as quietly as possible, Grandma still hears her. It seems that those glasses of sherry haven't done their work properly.

'Is that you, Elsie?' Grandma calls out.

'Yes,' Elsie answers. 'I'm just going to the toilet.'

But Elsie isn't really going to the toilet. Slowly and carefully she walks down the stairs, takes her coat from the hallstand, and opens the front door very quietly. She sits on the step and puts on her coat and shoes.

It is still quite dark and a greyish-blue mist is hanging in the air. In front of her, a brown snail is crawling across the tiles.

'Hello, snail,' says Elsie. 'Which way shall I go now?'

But the snail doesn't say anything of course. He has his own problems, even though he carries a home on his back.

# Willemine and the highwaymen

## 1. Willemine

On the day that Willemine went into the wide world, the sun was shining beautifully, butterflies were dancing in the air and the newspaper boy was whistling something by Mozart.

In her saddlebag she had bread with cucumber and cheese in a little box, two apples, two packets of liquorice allsorts, a jersey, a raincoat, an empty notebook, a felt-tip pen and a packet of sticking plasters.

A light southerly wind was blowing and so she rode towards the north, beside the canal.

The going was good. The bicycle tyres sang a barely audible melody on the tarmac, the handlebars sparkled in the morning sun, and the water fowl dived upside-down in the water as she passed. Willemine thought to herself: 'If I carry on at this rate, I'll be at the North Pole in no time at all!'

She cycled past a boat that was called the *Anna Jacoba* and was moving much more slowly than she was.

But some time later, when she was sitting on the grass beside the canal, the boat came puffing past *her* and she thought: 'And now it's my turn to ride past him . . .'

She laughed and took out her notebook. She wrote:

I am sitting on the grass.
White flowers are growing
here with orange
betles on them.
A boat is sailing
past, the ANNA
JACOBA. It is pulling
a little boat along behind
and it is called BRAM.
A seagull is sitting
on it and is sailing along
too, the lazybones,
the clever-clogs.

She crossed out clever-clogs because she wasn't sure if it had one g or two. She couldn't remember having that word at school but she didn't want to think about school now. It was a holiday, she was going into the wide world and she might never come back again, or perhaps she might later on, when she was grown up . . .

Yes, she'd come home again then, tanned by the sun, and everyone would look at her. After much hemming and hawing they would ask her to tell them about her adventures.

She would pause for a moment and then say: 'Wait until my book is published, all my experiences are in that. The first chapter is about my departure, how I cycled away from home with hardly anything at all in my saddlebag: just some bread, two apples, and a few sticking plasters . . . And the next twenty chapters describe all my adventures in detail: my journey across the Egyptian desert, when I always travelled at night, by the light of the moon. And my weary journey through the jungle, where everything was hot and humid and green and you could only make headway very slowly. You have to use your knife to hack your way through branches and creepers all the time and sometimes you accidentally cut straight through a snake that's just about to sink its poisonous fangs into you. All the chapters are about breathtaking adventures like those.'

RAILWAY LINE

CANAL

BRAM

ANNA JACOBA

CYCLE TRACK

DIKE

DIKE

And everyone who read the book would say: 'Can this really be the story of little Willemine who was always so timid and who always got low marks for sums? How on earth could she work out how to make a journey like that?'

She would provide the book with maps and drawings, and this was why she stopped now and made a clear drawing of the canal as she sat beside it.

## 2. Highwaymen

'Right then, so we're highwaymen,' shouted Leo Hengst. 'And our hideout's here in the bushes.' He planted a stick in the ground. A piece of red cloth was knotted to one end. 'Our hideout's here by this flag and I'm your chief.'

'Hooray for our chief!' shouted the others.

'Hoy!' shouted Leo.

'Hoy!' echoed the others.

'Hoy is our battle cry,' said Leo Hengst. 'Whenever I shout "Hoy" then you all have to shout too.'

He shouted 'Hoy' a couple of times, and the others shouted too as loudly as they could.

The others were:

Robert and Martin Wagenaar. They were brothers and both of them wore glasses and had put spots on their faces with a black felt-tip pen. The spots were supposed to look like stubble. They had sticks and cap guns tucked into their belts. They looked very fierce.

Lofty van Pelt. He was called Lofty because he

really was very tall. He was wearing a raincoat with a belt tied around it very tightly so that he looked extra thin. He had his hands in his pockets. He said that he knew how to handle plastic explosives and that he was an expert at derailing trains.

Leo Hengst didn't think that highwaymen derailed trains. 'I don't think that highwaymen derail trains,' he said. But Van Pelt told him that he didn't know what he was talking about.

Benny Bouwsens from Canal Street wanted to join the gang of highwaymen too, even though he didn't

really know what a highwayman was. He thought it was someone who repaired the highway. And that's why he laughed at Lofty van Pelt for thinking that highwaymen derailed trains by laying plastic explosives on the lines. 'Yukyuk . . .' he laughed.

'Stop laughing like that,' said Van Pelt.

And so Benny Bouwsens stopped laughing because he was only nine and a bit small and plump, a flea compared with Lofty van Pelt.

'Hey man, I could blow you away, just like that,' Van Pelt always said to him. And he said it again now.

'Stop your quarrelling,' Leo Hengst said firmly. 'We must all work together and help each other. We've got to be a gang of robbers and everyone must be scared of us. We'll go out and rob round about here. On the dyke and the canal.'

'If a train comes, I'm going to blow it up,' said Van Pelt.

'You'd do better blowing up a boat,' said Robert, who was busy drawing a moustache under Benny Bouwsens' nose with a black felt-tip pen. 'It's great when boats explode, they burn for a while and then they sink slowly to the bottom . . .'

'You must be crazy,' said Van Pelt. 'You don't know the first thing about plastic bombs. I'd have to swim out to the boat and the water's as cold as anything.'

'Yukyuk, you've got your raincoat on, haven't you?' laughed Benny.

'Watch it, you,' warned Lofty, 'or I'll blow you away . . .'

'Keep still,' Robert said to Benny. 'Your moustache is all crooked now.' He tried to straighten the moustache but it ended up looking like an ink blot on Benny's face.

'Make his face black all over,' said Martin.

But when Robert tried to do this, Benny backed away.

'I don't want any fooling around,' said Leo. 'We're not going out to rob any old how. We've got to draw up a plan. Now listen carefully to your chief and take careful note of everything I say. Nothing must go wrong. Point number one. Martin and Robert will go out as scouts first of all. Robert will go north along the canal and Martin will go south. They must look as inconspicuous as possible. Point number two. As soon as they see a lonely traveller, walker or jogger, they must report to Lofty, who will be the lookout and can decide if it's worth attacking the traveller and robbing him or taking him prisoner. Point number three . . .'

'That's a very good plan,' said Van Pelt. 'I'll hide behind the bushes on the dyke. The password is Plastic Bomb.'

'Him and his plastic bombs,' said Benny.

'Plastic Bomb is a very good password,' Leo decided. 'And it's a brilliant plan. Van Pelt will hide in the bushes up there on the dyke. And I'll stay here in the hideout and wait for the signal to go into action. Then I'll decide which weapons we'll use.'

'And what about me?' asked Benny. 'Where shall I go?'

'You'll stay here,' said Leo. 'I've got other plans for

26

you **and** you'll get special orders. You're just a beginner, anyway.'

'What do you mean?' Benny protested. 'I've been a robber just as long as the rest of you. You're either a robber or you're not . . .'

'Hark at him!' shouted Van Pelt. 'He only came along to watch. He didn't even know what a highwayman was. I'd like to know who *he's* attacked and who *he's* robbed.'

'I haven't noticed *you* doing much robbing either,' Benny said.

'You don't know what we get up to at night, laddie,' said Van Pelt.

There was no answer to that and so, while the others went out to scout or hide in their lookout post, Benny had to stay at the hideout and cut the grass with his penknife.

'And clear away all those thorns and nettles and thistles too,' Leo ordered as he neatly coiled a length of rope. 'I don't want anything to stick in my back if I decide to lie down here for a bit.'


## 3. The raid

By the time Willemine had finished her drawing, the boat was a good deal further down the canal and the water was calm once more. She ate one last sweet and then said to her bicycle, which was lying on the grass: 'Come on, you've had a nice long rest. We're going on again now, into the wide world.'

The bicycle had indeed had a good rest, or so it seemed, for it was eager to go and Willemine whizzed

27

along the canal bank. She was hoping to overtake the *Anna Jacoba* again and she sang a little song with a lot of talirralirras in it.

But she never caught up with the boat.

She stopped singing when she saw two boys running anxiously up and down ahead of her. They came running down the dyke first of all, and she thought: 'They're going to jump into the canal.' But they came to a stop right at the very edge. They pointed in her direction and then ran back up the dyke and vanished among some hawthorn bushes that were covered with white flowers. The bushes had a heavy scent and looked very pretty but there was something mysterious about them too, thanks to the disappearance of the boys.

Willemine grasped her bicycle handlebars more tightly, for the two boys might reappear at any moment. She didn't want to crash into them and cause an accident that would bring her journey round the world to an abrupt end . . .

Then, all at once, not two but four boys came yelling out of the bushes and tumbled down the dyke. They had sticks and rope, and they blocked the path so that she had to stop.

'Halt!' one of them shouted. He was clearly the leader. 'Stop!'

He said this even though she was already standing still.

'I've already stopped,' she said.

'Don't be so cheeky, you,' said the boy, who was holding a big stick that he thumped on the ground

28

every now and then. 'Get off that bike.'

Instead of getting off, Willemine turned the bike round and tried to ride away. But this didn't work: a tall grinning idiot in a raincoat was blocking the path behind her. The others tugged at her saddlebag.

'When we say get off that bike, we mean get off that bike,' the boy said again.

'Shall I slash the tyres?' asked a little twerp with dirty black marks under his nose. He was brandishing a penknife.

'Have you gone crazy?' said the tall one in the raincoat. 'If you're going to do stupid things like that then we'd better take that knife away from you right now. You don't go around cutting up the things you're trying to steal! We can really use a bike like this.'

'And there are all sorts of things in the bag,' said one of the boys in glasses, who had opened the saddlebag. 'Look, apples and liquorice allsorts.'

'Get away from that!' shouted the one who seemed to be in charge. 'We'll divide everything up properly in a minute.'

'Oh no you won't,' said Willemine.

'Oh yes we will,' said the boy in the raincoat. 'You don't seem to realize who we are and what's going on. This is a raid and we're highwaymen. We earn our living from what we can steal and that's why we attack travellers. We take all their things and beat them up or take them prisoner.'

'And this time it's your turn,' said the boy in charge. 'Tie her up and bring her to my hideout by the red flag.'

29

'Hoy!' the boys shouted and they grabbed Willemine, dragged her from the bicycle and threw a rope around her.

Willemine fought wildly and managed to graze her elbow on the tarmac as she did so. 'Ouch!' she yelled and then shouted: 'Stop! I give in! I'm your prisoner.'

They were delighted when she said that, and they took her in triumph to the hideout where they tied her up as if she was a joint of beef.

Willemine lay quietly on the grass that Benny had trimmed so neatly, trying to get her breath back. She gazed up at the sky and thought: 'This is my first adventure. Let's hope they don't throw away my notebook so I'll be able to write it all down . . .'

## 4. Benny Bouwsens and the sweets

Benny scratched at the earth with his penknife and stared at the girl, who was lying on her back and looking up at the sky. There was nothing at all to be seen in the sky. He was supposed to guard her and make sure that she didn't get up to any tricks.

He listened to the noise that the others were making on the dyke and behind it. He wondered what they were doing and longed to be with them.

'Why have you got those black marks on your face?' asked the girl, sitting up.

'It's felt-tip,' said Benny, feeling a little embarrassed. He must look really stupid. He remembered how they'd sniggered when they drew the moustache. They were always teasing him. He plunged his knife fiercely into the ground a couple of times.

'Those black stripes look awful,' she said. 'As if you've fallen on your face in the dirt, in soot or something like that.'

Benny rubbed his nose with his sleeve.

'It's still there,' said the girl. 'Try doing it with spit.'

'Oh, shut up,' said Benny.

The girl blew an insect away from her nose. 'It sounds to me as though those friends of yours are eating my apples and sweets,' she said. 'Hadn't you better go and see what they're doing?'

Benny stared at her. Her eyes were as blue as the sky. She could well be right. He wouldn't put it past them to eat the lot and leave nothing for him. After all, they'd called him 'laddie' and 'just a beginner' . . .

'If you try and escape you'll be for it,' Benny said as he stood up.

'Don't worry, I can't move,' said the girl. 'The rope is so tight that I couldn't even take one step.' She wiggled her feet but they were firmly knotted together.

'I'll be back in a minute,' said Benny. 'So stay exactly where you are now. If you've moved even one centimetre by the time I come back then you won't see your next birthday.'

'I'll stay right here, really I will,' the girl answered. 'It's nice here in the sun, out of the wind.' She lay back and shut her eyes, but when he turned round to look back at her, one eye was open again.

Benny crawled through the grass up the dyke with the knife between his teeth. He peered at the others from behind a bush. They were busy eating something and just then Lofty van Pelt threw an apple core into the canal.

Leo was sitting on the girl's bike; he rode down the dyke, shouting at the top of his voice, and screeched to a halt on the tarmac below. The cycle track was only a few metres wide.

'My turn, my turn!' shouted Robert and Martin.

'I want another sweet!' Leo shouted and passed the bicycle to the Wagenaar brothers. They at once began to squabble over it.

It looked as though they had taken the saddlebag off earlier and thrown it down. Now Leo walked towards it and searched inside for a sweet.

'You've eaten the lot!' he yelled. 'Who's got them?'

It turned out that Lofty van Pelt had taken the sweets, and so Leo Hengst was forced to chase after him.

Robert and Martin began to push the bicycle up the dyke together.

'Blast!' swore Benny, although it sounded quite different because of the knife between his teeth. He made his way back to the hideout.

The girl had been as good as her word. She was still lying exactly where he had left her.

'And?' she asked.

'What do you mean, and?' Benny asked dolefully.

'They've eaten everything, haven't they?' the girl said.

'They're mucking about with your bike,' said Benny. 'They're riding up and down the dyke. And they've taken the saddlebag off. They kept some of the sweets for me. I'll get them if I guard you properly.'

'Don't tell me you believed that,' said the girl. 'It looks to me as though they'd like to see the back of you.'

'Of course they don't,' said Benny.

'Oh yes, they do,' said the girl. 'Otherwise they wouldn't leave you here to guard a stupid girl. I bet they always give you the stupid things to do.'

'Shut your face,' said Benny.

He was getting tired of all this talking.

'Untie the rope a bit, will you?' the girl said after a while.

'I'm not mad, you know,' Benny said, cleaning his penknife on the grass.

33

'You're scared of the others,' she said.

'No, I'm not.'

'Then why don't you untie me? Not all the way, just so that I can get a packet of sweets out of my pocket. You can have them if you want. I've only had one so far. There must be at least nine left.'

Benny liked the sound of this. Not only would he get some sweets but it would also be a bit like robbing someone. He loosened the rope here and there and pulled the packet of sweets from her trouser pocket.

'Aren't I going to get one too?' she asked, and opened her mouth wide. Benny popped a sweet inside. The mouth closed immediately.

'Mmmmmmmmmmm,' she said.

Benny crammed three or four sweets into his mouth at once.


## 5. The letter

'What have you got in your mouth?' Leo asked Benny.

Benny tried to swallow the sweets as quickly as he could. He was sorry now that he'd put four of them in his mouth at the same time.

'Let's have a look,' said Leo, taking hold of Benny's chin. 'What's that black stuff?'

'It's felt-tip,' said Benny, trying to get free.

'You know what I mean,' said Leo. 'Open your mouth. I can smell liquorice. Where did you get it from? Spit it out!'

Benny spat in Leo's direction.

'You'll pay for that!' Leo shouted. 'Grab him, men!'

The others had arrived with Leo and now eagerly grabbed hold of Benny.

'Search his pockets!'

'They're in my hand,' Benny shouted. 'Here!' He opened his hand and Lofty van Pelt took the rest of the packet of sweets.

Van Pelt had stuck the plasters all over his face. It looked as though he'd just been shaving for the very first time.

'There are only two left,' he said.

'He's lying,' shouted Benny. 'There should be at least five left. Yes, definitely five.'

'Shut up,' said Leo. 'What shall we do with him?'

'Let's throw him in the canal,' said Van Pelt.

'We can do that any time,' said Leo. 'Let's tie him up first and then we can decide how we're going to punish him.'

'We haven't got any rope left,' said Robert Wagenaar. 'We only had one piece and we tied *her* up with that.'

'I won't run away, really I won't,' said Willemine. 'I think it's really nice here. Untie me.'

'Why should we untie you now?' asked Leo Hengst.

'Because you won't be able to tie *him* up if you don't,' she answered.

'We could tie them to each other, of course,' said Martin. He thought this was a really good idea. It made him laugh, anyway.

'Has anyone found a notebook?' Willemine asked.

'It's a blue notebook, without any lines. It was almost completely empty.'

'Is this what you mean?' asked Lofty van Pelt. He took a rolled-up notebook from his raincoat pocket. He opened the notebook and read what Willemine had written.

'Yes, that's the one,' said Willemine. 'I'm going to write down everything that happens. If you untie me, then I can write down your adventures: a story about a gang of bandits who capture a little girl and drag her to their cave . . .'

'We're not a gang of bandits,' said Leo. 'We're highwaymen.'

'The story of the highwaymen . . . That sounds really good,' said Willemine.

'It's not such a bad idea,' said Van Pelt, producing Willemine's felt-tip pen from his other pocket. 'Leo, if I were you I'd give the order for that girl to be untied and for our fat friend Benny to be tied up instead. Then she can write down our story and she can draw pictures too.'

'O.K.,' said Leo. 'But if she runs away then she'll really get what for.'

'What will we do then?' asked Martin.

'I won't run away, really I won't,' said Willemine.

Leo untied her and Van Pelt grabbed Benny by the hair because he had started to make a terrible fuss as soon as he'd heard that he was going to be tied up.

'Tie him up,' said Leo.

And so it was done.

Benny squealed like a pig having an injection and made all sorts of other noises that can't possibly be written down. He was shouting not so much because the rope was hurting him but more because he felt that he was being treated unfairly. After all, he had done his best to be a good highwayman and now they were pulling his hair and tying him up as if he didn't really belong to the gang! He wriggled like a worm, and twisted and turned. He wanted to be free, free, free.

But the others only laughed at him and made splendid knots in the rope, as if he was a parcel being sent by ship to Tasmania.

Willemine turned a couple of somersaults and then sat down, opened her notebook and began to write the story of the highwaymen.

# CHAPTER 1
# THE ROBBERS

'Right then!' said Leo. 'My name's Leo and I'm the chief robber. And the tall guy with the raincoat is called Van Pelt.'

'The explosives expert,' Van Pelt added.

'The explosives expert,' Benny mimicked.

'Shut him up!' Leo shouted.

Robert tied the red robber flag round Benny's mouth. He bit and puffed and snorted.

Willemine drew portraits of the different high-waymen and wrote their names underneath.

Then she started on the story.

V.P    L.HENGST    WAGENAAR bros.    BENNY B.

# There was once a gang of highwaymen

'You could ask for ransom money, you know,' said Willemine.

'What do you mean, ransom money?' asked Leo, who was looking at what she had written down.

'Well, we could write a letter to Benny's father and mother,' Willemine explained. 'We'll say that we've captured him and that they can have him back if they pay us ten thousand guilders.'

'You must be joking!' laughed Van Pelt. 'Ten thousand guilders for that little creep? They'd just say: You can keep him, boys. He's just not worth it!'

'Well, a thousand guilders then,' Willemine suggested.

'That seems a fair enough figure to me,' said Leo.

'Benny's father and mother aren't very rich,' Robert said.

'A hundred guilders then,' said Willemine.

'That's better,' said Van Pelt. 'One hundred guilders. That'll be twenty-five guilders each.'

'All right then, write the letter,' Leo said to Willemine.

And she wrote:

We have captured your
son he is in
a secret place
if you want him back
you must pay us
100 guilders. You must
not tell the police.
from a secret sender
but
WE MEAN BUSINESS

'Who's going to deliver the letter?' asked Leo.

'We'll do it,' said Robert and Martin. 'We've got to be home for dinner anyway and we go along Canal Street.'

Willemine tore the page out of her notebook, folded it tightly, and gave it to the brothers.

'You'd better make sure that no one sees you,' Leo warned.

'His parents won't be at home,' said Martin. 'They both go out to work.'

'They never come home at dinner time,' said Robert.

'I repeat: make sure no one sees you,' said Leo. 'It must all be done very carefully. The neighbours mustn't notice anything because if they recognize you it'll all go wrong and we'll have the police on our trail before we know where we are.'

'They won't recognize my handwriting, anyway,' said Willemine. 'At least we can show them that we mean business.'

She had noticed Benny's penknife lying in the grass where it had fallen during the struggle, and now she picked it up. She opened the knife and walked towards Benny. He stared wide-eyed with fright at the girl coming towards him with a gleaming knife in her hand.

'You're not going to stab him, are you?' Leo asked.

Willemine didn't stab Benny. Instead she cut a generous lock of his hair. 'Here,' she said to Robert and Martin. 'Put this in the letter, then they'll see that we've really captured their son and that we'll stop at nothing.'

Then Robert and Martin left with the letter into which the lock of hair was folded. 'We'll be back at about two o'clock,' they said.

'I've got to go home too,' said Leo. 'It's half past twelve already.'

'A fine bunch of highwaymen, I must say!' Van Pelt said scornfully. He had pulled the flagpole out of the ground and was slashing the hawthorn bushes with it. 'I suppose I'll have to guard these two on my own,' he grumbled.

'I'll be back in about an hour,' Leo said and disappeared into the bushes.

Willemine pretended to be writing busily in her notebook but she kept a close eye on Van Pelt.

He stopped hitting the bushes after a while. He obviously found it much too tiring. He flung the flagpole into the bushes as if it were a javelin, and then he too vanished among the hawthorns. The thorns didn't trouble him much because of his raincoat.

Willemine began to cut Benny free.


## 6. Into the wide world

Willemine was cycling beside the canal with Benny on the back.

Benny was holding the saddlebag on his knees. He turned to look behind them. 'You needn't pedal so fast any more,' he said. 'Van Pelt is much too lazy to chase us.'

'Can you still see him?' Willemine asked.

'Yes, he's standing on the dyke watching us. He's

got his hands in his pockets. He usually has his hands in his pockets. He says that he knows all about plastic explosives and bombs.'

'He's no friend of yours,' said Willemine. She started to pedal more slowly. She had lost a lot of time, thanks to this business with the so-called high-waymen. And her apples had gone. And the liquorice allsorts too.

But the sun was shining and the wind was in the right direction. The water in the canal was sparkling, and she had already had an adventure that she had written down neatly in her notebook. If adventures happened at this rate then the notebook would be full in a few days' time and it was still only the afternoon of the first day.

'Where exactly are you going?' asked Benny.

'Me?' answered Willemine. 'I'm going into the wide world. Though I'm not going to get very far with a fatty like you on the back.'

# Witch

'That's where she lives, at number thirteen.' Little Vera nodded towards a tall, narrow house crammed between 'The Cigar Palace' and the electrical shop called 'Modern Light'.

Harry could see nothing special about the house. It was built of grey brick and had a dark green, almost black door with a knocker in the shape of a hand holding an apple. A nameplate was screwed to the doorpost under the bell push. It read: *Natalia Rozanova*.

'Rozanova,' said Harry, rolling the letter R. 'Rrrr.' And he repeated the name a couple of times.

'Ssh,' said Little Vera. 'Not so loud. Someone might hear you. I thought I saw the curtain move and . . .'

Beside the door there was a window. The curtains were drawn and motionless.

'Rozanova,' Harry said again.

'That's the witch's name,' Little Vera said softly. She grabbed Harry's arm and pulled him away.

Harry could feel her sharp little nails through his sleeve.

'You should try cutting your nails some time,' he said.

'Quiet,' Little Vera hissed. 'Try and look as natural as possible. And don't turn round or else she'll put the Evil Eye on you . . .'

'What happens then?' Harry asked. He was glad that Little Vera was only pulling at his shirt now. He felt sure there must be five red scratches on his skin.

'Then you'll be bewitched,' Little Vera went on. 'She's got one good eye and one Evil Eye and that's as nasty as anything. She only needs to look at you once with it and something awful will happen to you.'

'Like what?' asked Harry. He pulled himself free of Little Vera's grasp.

'You have to do exactly what she tells you. If she wants you to go to her then you have to do it, just like that. Whether you like it or not.'

'That's really something!' said Harry.

'Even if you were a hundred kilometres away, at the Panama Canal or somewhere, you'd still have to go to her.'

'The Panama Canal is in Central America,' said Harry. 'It joins the Atlantic Ocean and the Pacific Ocean.'

'So what?' asked Little Vera.

'So what? It's much more than a hundred kilometres away,' said Harry.

'That's neither here nor there,' Little Vera went on. 'You'd still go. You'd go straight to her, no matter what. You'd just drop everything and go. Even if you were eating a piece of cake, say, a piece of cream cake with fruit on it and little bits of chocolate and those tiny silver things, and if she wanted you to go to her you'd just drop your fork and leave the cake where it was and go straight to her. You wouldn't even take another bite, you wouldn't even finish what you've got in your mouth, you'd just *go*.'

'Wow!' said Harry. He was very fond of cream cake with little bits of chocolate on it.

'Even if you were lying in bed, fast asleep, and she called you, you'd get up right away and go to her in your pyjamas and bare feet. You'd walk straight through ditches and thorn bushes and barbed wire . . .'

'But what if the door's locked?' asked Harry, who didn't like the idea of walking around barefoot. And he didn't like the sound of that barbed wire either.

'You'd still carry on,' said Little Vera. 'If the door was locked, you'd kick it down and *then* go to her.'

'I can just see me kicking a door down in my bare feet,' said Harry. 'It wouldn't work, if you ask me.'

'Well, you'd do it just the same,' Little Vera said. 'It would hurt a lot, of course, and you'd get cuts and splinters everywhere but you'd do it and go to her, come what may.'

'And then what?' asked Harry. He never slept with his bedroom door locked.

'It all depends,' said Little Vera. 'Come on, we'll walk slowly down the street and then walk back up on the other side. Then we'll go into the pet shop. It's right opposite number thirteen. She won't be able to tell that we're keeping an eye on her.'

Harry and Little Vera walked down the street and then turned back. Cars were parked on both sides and they were able to keep out of sight behind them.

'Natalia Rozanova,' said Harry. 'How do you know she's a witch?'

'You can tell just by looking at her,' said Little Vera. 'There are all sorts of other signs too. She's run away from her husband . . .'

'What's that got to do with it?' asked Harry. 'That happens all the time. Women run away from their husbands every day.'

'You didn't let me finish,' said Little Vera. 'Of course they do, I know that. But when *she* ran away she put on a black dress to write a farewell letter and she threw her wedding ring down the toilet. And when she burned the photos of her husband he got a terrible pain all over as if someone had splashed petrol over him and set light to it. He rolled around on the floor groaning but you couldn't see any flames.'

'How do you know?' asked Harry. He could feel the little hairs on his arms standing on end.

'My mother told me and she heard about it from the lady next door. She's worn nothing but black ever since she left her husband. Her hair's turned grey from sorrow and her lips and nails are always painted black. One of her eyes is black, too, and the other one's green.'

'And that's the Evil Eye,' said Harry.

'No, the black one is, stupid,' said Little Vera. 'You obviously don't know the first thing about witches.'

They went into 'Everything For Your Pet' to see if it lived up to its name. They squeezed the rubber bones and shoes for dogs to chew and rummaged through the tins of animal food.

'Cat meat isn't really cat meat,' said Little Vera, taking a tin of Whiskas from the shelf and reading the label. She miaowed and put the tin back. The cat on the label grinned back at her. 'She's got a couple of cats too,' said Little Vera. 'Black ones, of course.'

'So there's a good chance that she comes in here to buy things every now and then,' said Harry.

'Well, no,' said Little Vera. 'She hardly ever comes out during the day. She only comes out in the middle of the night. And she gives those cats a different kind of food . . .' She didn't say what sort of food witch's cats *did* eat but just smiled a mysterious smile.

Harry didn't want to hear any more nasty stories. From time to time he glanced through the shop window under 'Ǝverything For Your Pet' at the house with the number thirteen but nothing happened.

They wandered around the shop for a while. They opened and closed a few birdcages and made sure that the dog leads were strong enough; they noticed that some of them had nasty spikes underneath to keep the animals under control. When they started to ring the cat bells, the shopkeeper came over to ask if he could help them.

'I'd like a guilder's worth of water plants for my fish,' said Little Vera. 'He's eaten everything up.'

Following Little Vera's directions, the man fished a green string from a water tank and put it in a small plastic bag.

Little Vera took a guilder from her pocket and then they couldn't stay in the shop any longer because the man said, 'Good day to you,' very firmly indeed.

They took another look at the aquarium with goldfish in it. There was a castle on the bottom with windows and doors for the fish to swim in and out. But they weren't doing that.

'Since when have you had a fish?' Harry asked. Each time he'd been to Little Vera's bedroom it had always been in a terrible mess with all sorts of things lying about, but he had never seen a fishtank there or anything like it.

49

'I haven't got one,' said Little Vera.

'So why did you buy a water plant?'

'I couldn't think of anything else,' said Little Vera, 'and we couldn't have hung around that shop for much longer.'

'It was all a waste of time, anyway,' said Harry. 'Especially if she never comes out of the house during the day. How do you know she's at home now?'

'Believe me, she is,' said Little Vera. 'I saw the curtain move. She's been watching us all the time. Come on, we'll walk slowly up the other side.'

Little Vera took the plant out of the plastic bag and laid it between her nose and upper lip. 'A moustache,' she said, but because the water dripped down her chin she left the plant on the roof of one of the cars they passed. Then she proceeded to blow up the bag in order to burst it.

'If that Rozanova gets her hands on you, you won't live to see another birthday,' she said between puffing and banging. 'She'll shut you in an electrified steel cage and burn all your hair off. And if she doesn't like you, she'll give you bread full of worms to eat or yoghurt with glass in it or mince with sawdust.'

'And what if she *does* like you?' asked Harry, who thought that yoghurt with glass in it sounded very nasty indeed.

'Then you get really nice food,' said Little Vera. 'Soup mainly, and garlic to purify the blood, because after a while she'll cut your toes off and drain all your blood. She needs it for her bath and to drink, too . . .'

'I don't believe any of this,' said Harry, thinking of a bath filled with blood.

'Well, don't then,' said Little Vera. She gave up trying to burst the bag and walked on in a huff. 'Do you really think that I'd make up something like that just to make a fool of my best friend, because that's what you are, you know. Go and see for yourself if you don't believe me.'

'Now, now,' Harry said, trying to calm her down.

'Now, now, nothing,' answered Little Vera. 'Come and take a look for yourself.'

Once again Harry felt those nasty little nails on his arm. Little Vera led him down a narrow alleyway between low walls and black tarred fences to the back of number thirteen, the narrow house where the witch Natalia Rozanova was supposed to live.

'You go inside. I'll wait here,' said Little Vera. 'If anything happens to you I can always go and get your mother and the police and the ambulance. If anything does happen, start yelling right away, O.K.?'

'O.K.,' said Harry.

They were standing by a rough fence of black wood. There was a gate in it that seemed to be locked. Little Vera helped Harry over the fence. They didn't say anything else and when Harry lowered himself from the fence into the garden it seemed as though a cloud of silence had fallen from the sky.

The garden was small and badly neglected. Here and there tall weeds stuck out of the ground. In the middle stood an overgrown lilac tree with dark purple flowers. Harry could see some of those insects that hang in the air for a while before suddenly darting away.

Ducking down behind the bushes, Harry made his

51

way towards an extension to the house that turned out to be a perfectly ordinary kitchen.

When at last he found himself inside, the blood was pounding in his head and he had to swallow hard a couple of times. But there was no sign anywhere of dried rats, bats or frogs, and there were no bottles of poison or ground bones either. On a table lay some small change, a brown loaf and a packet of chocolate flakes. And on the stove there were no mysterious cooking pots filled with blue-green smoke, just a saucepan in which some brown beans were soaking. They lay quietly in the water, looking a bit wrinkled. The kitchen didn't seem at all creepy. Neither did the hall he came to next. The only strange object there was a copper umbrella stand with a teddy bear in it, but even that wasn't *really* odd.

Harry realized then how strange it was that, in spite of all Little Vera's stories, he should actually have gone inside an unknown house, that he should actually have gone into someone else's kitchen and seen their chocolate flakes and brown beans. And that he should then have walked into the hall and slowly turned the handle of a door and carefully pushed it open . . .

Behind the door was a dimly lit room full of furniture. Through a gap in the curtains peeped a beam of sunlight in which specks of dust were dancing. A bluebottle buzzed mournfully behind the curtain.

The beam of light fell straight on to a gleaming black piano. There was a sheet of music on the stand. And then something flew past Harry's shoulder and

53

landed on the piano, knocking the sheet of paper to the floor. It was a cushion that had been thrown at Harry and now fell on the carpet with a dull thud.

Harry turned round but he could see and hear nothing. The piano made a gentle ringing sound. Harry gasped for breath and felt the hairs on his arms tingling once again.

Then he heard a soft giggling coming from behind a chair and shortly after that a little girl appeared. 'Hello,' she said. 'Have you come to play with me?'

She was a lot smaller and younger than Harry, about six or seven years old, he guessed. She was wearing a nightie with a vest over the top that was much too big for her.

'My mother says I mustn't go out,' she said. 'I've been ill. Shall I play you something on the piano?'

Before Harry could say anything, she had sat down at the piano and played a few hundred notes with her nimble little fingers.

'Diabelli,' she said, and then: 'Aren't you going to clap?'

'Am I supposed to?' Harry asked and applauded.

'Only if you liked it,' she answered.

Then she played something else with a lot of very high notes. And Harry clapped once again when it was finished.

'Did you like that one too? I made it up all by myself.'

Harry was feeling very uneasy. He could hardly spend the whole afternoon listening to a little girl playing the piano while Little Vera stood waiting outside. She was bound to have heard the music too.

Besides, Mrs Rozanova might come home at any moment. She might even be upstairs now . . . Harry went hot all over at the thought.

'Can you play the piano too?' the little girl asked. She turned round on the piano stool and looked him straight in the eyes.

'No,' said Harry. Her eyes were very dark.

'Do you want to learn?' she asked. She turned back to the piano and struck a note. 'That's the doh,' she said.

'I don't have much time just at the moment,' Harry said. But he didn't go away, even so.

'And do you write stories?' She stood up, crossed to the table and picked up a piece of paper on which the following was typed:

55

sto ry by
Lina Rozanova


Once there lived in 1 ood
a litle girl she lived all
alone in a cave and no
one gave her anything to eat
and so she only ate
roots and mushrooms and
beries
she as thin as 1 plank
she had never seen
bread
she ore 1 dress of skin
and she alked about in
bear feet
1 day a hunter came
he shot 1 arro in her
he thought that she
as an animal

'Do you think it's nice?'

'It isn't finished yet,' said Harry. 'And, er, there seem to be a few mistakes in it. What does alked mean?'

'Oh yes, it does have some typing mistakes,' said Lina. 'Typing is quite different from playing the piano. And the letter w doesn't work. But don't you think it's a nice story?'

'Yes, it's nice and exciting but what happens next?'

'The best bit is still to come,' said Lina. 'I'm going to make the little girl fall in love with the hunter. Don't you think that'll be nice?'

'Perhaps . . .' Harry hesitated.

'Of course it will,' said Lina. 'Are you in love with anybody?'

'Well, no, not really,' Harry answered. He ought to try and get away now. Little Vera was bound to be worried. She might think that he really *had* been locked up in a cage. Perhaps it wouldn't be such a bad thing if she *did* think that.

'Then we must fall in love,' said Lina. 'The two of us, all right?'

'It doesn't happen just like that,' said Harry.

'It can happen very quickly,' she said. 'Don't you know what it's like?'

'Yes, a little,' said Harry.

Luckily it was almost dark in the room and Little Vera wasn't there. He could tell his cheeks were red.

'It's a feeling,' she said. 'You always want to be with each other and give each other presents, and you write letters to each other and think about each other all the time . . .'

At that moment a lady came into the room. She said: 'Why on earth are you sitting in the dark on such a lovely day?'

She drew back the curtains.

The lady didn't have grey hair but black hair like Lina's, and she was wearing blue clothes. She stood and looked out of the window.

'There's someone on the fence,' she said.

Little Vera was sitting on the fence. She was waving and looking a little embarrassed.

'Who's that?' Lina asked. She looked at Harry with her black eyes.

'I don't know,' said Harry. He knew that his cheeks must be flaming red now.

'Yes, you do,' said Lina. 'The two of you have been spying on us all afternoon. You hid behind the cars and in the pet shop across the road . . . But from now on you and I . . .'

'Stop imagining things,' said the lady, who seemed to be Lina's mother. 'Go and wash now and get dressed properly.'

'All right, Mum, as long as he can come back to read my stories,' said Lina. 'And you've *got* to come back!' she said firmly to Harry, pointing at him with a white bony finger. 'You've got to come and play with me and you've got to learn to play the piano and we're going to write letters to each other . . .'

'You're very quiet,' Little Vera said as they walked down the street again a little later on. 'I've got a hole in my trousers from that fence. There was a nail and I got caught on it. I wanted to find out why you were taking such a long time and I heard someone tinkling on a piano. You don't play the piano, do you?'

'It wasn't tinkling,' said Harry. 'It was Diabelli and . . .' But he didn't say the name.

'Who was playing then?' asked Little Vera. 'Was she just like I said? Why won't you tell me anything? Did she get you with her Evil Eye? Why are you such a wet blanket all of a sudden?'

'Oh, push off!' said Harry. 'There's nothing there.'

'I told you so!' Little Vera shouted. But she didn't go away. She walked on beside him, covering the hole in her trousers with one hand.

# Lottie

A good ten years ago some children were playing beside the railway line. They were Maarten van Rooy, Inge de Bruin and Peter Swartjes. It was a Wednesday afternoon and the weather was fine. They were looking for round white pebbles to play shops with. And they put a coin on the rails and waited for the train. Soon enough it came. It rushed past, wailing angrily. Bits of paper and plastic cups came flying through the air. The children waved and shouted but the train was making far too much noise.

'Wow, wasn't it going fast?' Maarten shouted. 'That coin's squashed really flat.'

'Shut up a minute,' Inge said. 'I can hear something.'

As the roaring of the train died away, the others could hear something too.

'I know that sound, it's a cat,' said Peter. 'There's a cat in that bag.'

A little way off, a few metres from the rails, a rubbish bag was lying. Inside it was a little baby which began to cry with all its might when the children picked up the bag.

'It's just a little baby,' said Inge.

She took the baby out of the bag. It had a bare little head and it was wearing a very big T-shirt with an advertisement for bananas on it. It was very wet. Both the baby's legs were inside one man's checked sock.

'It's peed everywhere, ugh,' said Maarten, who was holding the baby now. 'These clothes are wet through.'

'Perhaps it fell out of the train,' said Peter. He couldn't see or hear the train any more.

'Or it may have been lying here for ages,' said Maarten. 'He's awfully cold, anyway.'

They wrapped the baby in Peter's jacket and took him away.

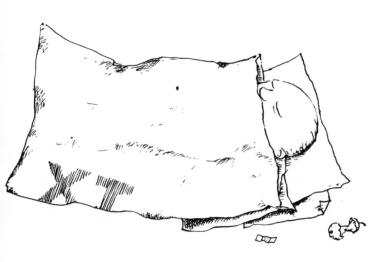

'What's your name?' Inge said to the baby.

'Don't be stupid,' said Maarten. 'It's only a baby. He doesn't know how to talk yet.'

'Seems to me that all he can do is cry,' said Peter.

'But how are we going to find out whose baby it is?' asked Inge.

No one ever found out. The child's parents were never traced. The baby that had been found by the railway line turned out to be a little girl. She was wearing only a man's shirt and a man's sock, and had been placed in a grey plastic rubbish bag measuring sixty centimetres by eighty with the letters XT on it. They named her Lottie.

Lottie grew up in a Children's Home, although she didn't grow very fast. She stayed on the small side, grew thin red hair, usually had a cold and a nose that was always running.

The people who ran the Home called her Lottie, but the children called her Snottie because of her runny nose and also because it rhymed with Lottie, of course.

For more than nine years Lottie stayed in that Home with other children who didn't have parents or whose parents couldn't look after them any more or just wanted to get rid of them.

It was a big house with many rooms and a dining hall. There was also a dormitory with iron beds and a cupboard for each child for clothes and other things.

Lottie had a lot of handkerchiefs in her cupboard and a little doll that she had made herself. She had cut two pieces of cloth in the shape of a doll, sewn them together, and filled this with scraps of wool and rags. Two buttons served as eyes and the hair was tufts of wool.

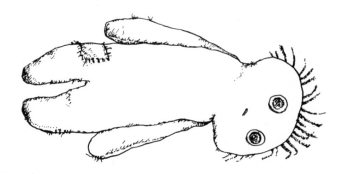

She named the doll Compie, simply because she thought it sounded nice. And she talked to it when she lay in bed. Quietly, because you weren't allowed to talk out loud.

'You shouldn't lie around sniffing and snivelling the whole time, Snottie Snotnose!' the other children said.

'I can't help it,' Lottie answered. 'I've always got a cold . . .'

'Serves you right for lying down by the railway line!' the other children shouted.

They were always teasing her. Sometimes they teased her so much that Lottie lay down and whimpered, pressing Compie to her cheek. That doll may have been no bigger than a grown-up's hand but it had seen a great deal of sorrow.

One beautiful October afternoon a lady and gentleman came to visit the Home. They had come to collect a child because they couldn't have one of their own. They chose Lottie, because the lady thought that she was so small and pathetic and sweet with that little red nose.

'You'd like to come home with us, wouldn't you?' the lady said. She put a plump warm arm round Lottie and drew her closer.

The lady's dress was covered with pink flowers and she smelt of flowers, too, even Lottie could smell them. The gentleman had a camera with him and he took photographs of the pretty scene.

As luck would have it, Miss Esther was there, the housemother. She said: 'Go to the dormitory and pack your things, and then you can go with the lady and gentleman in their car.'

And so Lottie went with them in a big beige car. She had to sit at the back on a soft seat with a suitcase beside her with clothes, handkerchiefs and Compie inside.

The gentleman sat behind the steering wheel and smoked a cigar. He wound the window down.

'Shut that window, Harry,' said the lady. 'We don't want Lottie to catch cold, do we?'

'I opened it because of the smoke,' said the gentleman.

'We don't mind that,' said the lady. She looked back at Lottie and smiled. She had a gold tooth. She must be a very rich lady, Lottie thought.

'Lottie,' said the lady. 'That's short for Charlotte, isn't it?'

'Yes, miss,' said Lottie. 'I think so . . . But they call me Lottie.'

She didn't mention that she was usually called Snottie. It would be best if these people didn't get to know that. She didn't want to give them any ideas. Just imagine if they started to call her that too . . .

'Do you think it's a nice name, Lottie?' the lady asked. 'Wouldn't you rather have a different name: Angélique or Josephine or something like that? Perhaps it would be a good idea if we called you something different from now on. We've got a list of names at home and you can choose one of those. A name that you really like. A girl's name, of course. We've also made a list of boys' names. The list of girls' names is longer, though. I'm sure there's one you'll like. There's bound to be. We turn left along here. You'll soon get used to it, I think. You've been in that Home for such a long time. You've got rather a cold, haven't you? Well, it's not surprising in a place like that. Soon you'll be able to have a lovely hot bath and then we'll have some chocolate milk to drink because you must be feeling really tired and then we'll go and buy some new clothes because we want you to look really nice. I think we'll put your hair in curls. That'll look really nice, won't it?'

'You ought to give the child time to settle down and get used to things,' said the gentleman.

'The sooner she forgets that Home the better,' the lady answered.

'You'll have a really beautiful room, anyway,' said the gentleman. Every now and then he puffed out clouds of smoke.

'Yes, it'll really make you sit up,' said the lady. 'We've done up a room specially just for you, and guess what colour the wallpaper is? Come on now, have a guess, Lottie.'

'I don't know . . .' said Lottie. 'Pink perhaps?'

'Did you hear that, Harry? Didn't I tell you? I knew pink was right. Little girls love pink.'

'I told you that you'd choose a girl,' said the gentleman.

'Here we are, behind those trees,' said the lady.

The car turned into a gravel drive and stopped outside a big house with lots of bay windows and a big brown door.

The walls of the room where Lottie found herself were swarming with pink flowers. Even the ceiling was covered with flowered paper.

The room looked like a pink forest. A lamp hung from the ceiling with a fringe round the shade. The bed had a cover with bobbles on, and on it were lying at least twenty cushions and a big doll that could cry and pee if you put water inside it. There was a little cord on her back, with a ring at the end. If you pulled it, the doll's head nodded and the eyes opened and closed.

An alarm clock was ticking on the bedside table. The head of Donald Duck on the clockface moved with each tick.

On the other side of the bed stood a bookcase, a chest full of toys and a big wardrobe with a mirror.

Lottie looked at herself. She looked strange in her frilly flowered dress and with masses of curls in her hair. She also had white socks on and black shiny shoes that gleamed like beetles.

'Well, you certainly look a lot different now, don't you, Lottie?' the lady said, surveying her with her head to one side. 'Turn round so that Harry can take a photo of you.'

'I can't use the flash because of the mirror,' said the gentleman, standing ready with the camera.

'Now you must be perfectly still and leave your nose alone. It'll soon be red all over from all that rubbing.'

'I haven't got a hankie, miss,' said Lottie. 'I've nowhere to keep it.'

'I'll get you a little bag,' said the lady. 'We'll buy a nice little handbag to match your shoes. And you really must stop calling me miss from now on. You can call me Mummy, if you like, but Judy would be nice too. That's my name. Judy. Whatever you like. There are hankies in the chest of drawers. I've thrown away the ones you brought with you. They were men's handkerchiefs and they were worn out, anyway. They were in shreds. Are you looking for something? Oh, your suitcase. You're looking for your case. I threw that away too.'

'But Compie was in it!' Lottie cried.

'Compie? Oh, you mean that dirty little doll. It was really filthy so I threw it in the dustbin. It was such a nasty little thing. You could catch something from it. Now don't look so bewildered. There's a lovely new doll on the bed for you to play with. If you put water inside, then she'll cry and go wee-wee. Here you are . . .'

She took the doll and thrust it into Lottie's arms.

It was a big, hard, stiff doll, with shiny nylon hair. She was almost as big as Lottie, a good ninety centimentres or more.

'If you give her a shake then she'll cry.' Mrs Judy showed Lottie how to shake the doll.

'Beeeeep,' went the doll, a harsh, monotonous complaint.

Lottie shook the doll herself, just once, and felt the long eyelashes. The eyes were blue.

'You're really going to love it here,' said the lady. 'And do wipe your nose or else the doll's hair will get all dirty. You really must learn to blow your nose in time.'

Lottie had a great deal to learn. She had to learn how to eat properly at a table with a snow-white cloth, without leaving any soup stains or spots of grease. She had to learn how to eat with a knife and fork without sticking her elbows in the air. And she had to learn to wipe her mouth with a napkin before taking a drink from her glass of mineral water. And she had to learn to drink tea in the correct way, that is to say by holding the saucer in one hand and the cup in the other, having first taken the spoon out of the cup and lain it in the saucer. She had to learn to eat a piece of cake with a pastry fork, without dropping the cake, and she had to learn to walk up the staircase one step at a time without kicking the brass stair-rods. Yes, she had a great deal to learn, but what else can you expect when you've been dragged out of a rubbish bag?

In the beginning Lottie searched the rubbish bags and pedal bins more than once to see if she could find any trace of Compie. But she'd been taken away long before, of course, and thrown on the rubbish tip.

She was given more and more dolls but none were like Compie. Mr Harry often brought her dolls and toys; her room was pretty well full of them and there were other things in the loft, too.

In her room she had a plump blue plush dog that she called Poopinette. And in a corner stood Bert and Ernie from Sesame Street and a chicken that hopped about if you wound it up. And a frog that could open its mouth and croak. There was also a tortoise house made of plastic. It consisted of an enormous tortoise with a shell that looked like a toadstool. There was a little door in it so that you could take toys out: little plastic tortoises, a slide, a dresser and a table for the little tortoises. She also had a china tea set, complete with a tray. And she had Cindy and Barbie dolls with roller skates. And a doll's head that you could put make-up on. You could wash and style the hair and there was a box of children's make-up and lilac nail varnish. And she had jigsaw puzzles with eight hundred and fifteen hundred pieces but you could see on the boxes what they were supposed to be: a landscape in Austria with lots of sky, and a big flower arrangement with butterflies on it.

And in the loft there was Play-mobil and Lego, and an illuminated globe to help find places in the world, a skateboard, a ping pong table, a wooden sledge with a back to it, a house telephone so that she could ring up her bedroom from the loft (except that there was no one there to answer it), a racetrack with two loops, a Viewmaster set, a compendium of games, a school desk with a cupboard full of felt-tip pens, note pads and other writing things.

Mr Harry had also given her roller skates with yellow wheels, and a bicycle, a hockey stick and a tennis racket, and she had to go to ballet classes and learn how to play the recorder and tennis. And he took photographs of her with the hockey stick and tennis racket. The photo of Lottie in her ballet dress didn't come out because she couldn't stand on one leg for long enough.

And she went to a school. Not to the one in the village but to a much better one, about fourteen kilometres further on. Mrs Judy took her there in the big beige car and collected her afterwards.

'I want to keep the name Lottie,' said Lottie.

Apart from this, Lottie didn't say very much. Though she often said, 'Thank you very much,' of course.

The mountain of toys continued to grow but she hardly ever played with them. She tried to reach low C on the recorder but she couldn't manage it, and she never poured water in the big doll and so it never wet itself. She wasn't allowed to roller skate indoors and she wasn't allowed on the road and you couldn't skate on the gravel drive.

'You don't say much, do you?' said Mrs Judy. 'And you hardly ever play. And you look so miserable and you don't eat much. It'll be Christmas soon and you'll have a lovely time then. You'll get presents. You must make a present list and write down all the things you would really like. You know what a present list is, don't you?'

'It's a letter to Father Christmas,' said Lottie, and she went up to the loft. There she sat down at the school desk and wrote a letter to Father Christmas. She stuffed the letter into her shoe and put it by the fireplace, where a fire burned so fiercely that no living soul could possibly pass through it. And she sang a little song she had learned in the Home: a song about a moon shining through the trees. And after that she went to bed.

Dear Father Christmas.
This is Lottie writing
to you.
Please Bring nothing.
I have Already Everything roller
skates and a bicycle
and a skateboard and dolls
and Everything.
Take it All Away but
Please bring
my Compie
back.
Your Lottie
Faithfully.

She hadn't been in bed very long when there came a knock at the door. It was not Father Christmas. It was Mrs Judy and Mr Harry. They switched on the light. They came and stood at the foot of the bed, looking very cross. Mrs Judy had the letter in her hand. She had crumpled it up a little.

'What's the meaning of this, then?' she asked. She was angry and sad. Both at the same time. Sometimes she was more angry than sad. 'What does this mean?' She waved the letter wildly, crumpling it even more. 'If this is anything to go by then you don't seem to realize just how much we've done for you. We took you out of that Home, gave you clothes, a lovely room,' (she pointed the letter at the walls of the room) 'piles of toys, the best wasn't good enough for you: shoes that cost two hundred guilders, a bicycle that cost three hundred. We let you go to music lessons but you still can't reach a low C. We sent you to the best school we could find and it seems that you've learned precious little there. Yes, that's right, start snivelling again. They didn't call you Snottie for nothing . . .'

Lottie began to cry very loudly.

Mr Harry didn't take a photo of her. He said: 'Perhaps you'd rather go back to that Home? You don't have to stay here, you know. If you want to go back you only need to say so. There are plenty of other children who'd be only too glad to come here and make the most of the opportunities we can offer them. Do you understand me? Well?'

This all sounded very angry.

'What do you say, then?'

The lady added more fuel to the flames.

'I want Compie back.' Lottie's voice squeaked. She was holding a handkerchief over her face. She wished that it could hide her completely.

'She wants *what*?' asked Mr Harry.

'She wants Compie back,' Mrs Judy answered. 'She means that disgusting doll. I threw it in the dustbin. It was the most awful rubbish.'

'How ridiculous!' said Mr Harry. 'She's absolutely hopeless. What an absurd state of affairs.'

And to Lottie he said: 'Well now, I've made myself perfectly clear. You may stay here tonight but you'll have to decide very carefully exactly what you want to do. You may stay on here but you'll have to do exactly as we say or else you'll go straight back to that Home. Is *that* what you want?'

Lottie was crying so much that she could only make strange noises.

The lady and the gentleman walked away. They put out the light. Lottie heard the lady say: 'She's such a difficult child, it must be her nature.'

Then the bedroom door closed.

That night Lottie ran away. She was found a few days later, near the railway line.

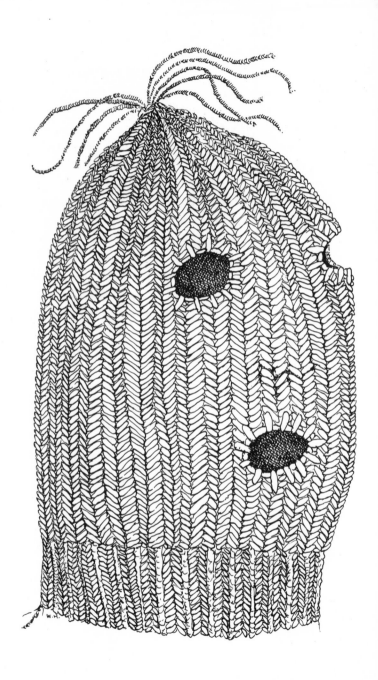

# Thieves

Henkie Visser was ten and Julie Snoep was nine. They were thieves. They stole ballpoint pens from the stationer's, they nicked shampoo and cough sweets from the chemist and they pinched dates, plums and pears from the greengrocer. Henkie even stuck a cucumber up his sleeve once.

They had taken an electric flashlight from a department store, and sticky tape, a glass head that you were supposed to put a Walkman on, and a whole lot of other things, because they often spent a lot of time in that shop.

It was Henkie who took most of the things and Julie helped him by talking to the shop assistant. Or keeping a lookout. She found this exciting. She had a mask of green wool that she could pull down over her face. There was a red tassel on the top that she had sewn on to it at school. She had edged the eyes with a buttonhole stitch. The mask looked really great but Julie had never used it when they were stealing.

'They'd recognize you right away in a stupid thing like that,' Henkie always said.

This time Henkie had taken a fondue set in a box from the department store. They stopped in a back street somewhere to inspect their loot. There was an enamel pan in the box with a picture of a tree with autumn leaves on it. There was also a black lid with a wooden knob, four metal forks and a little dish for the spirit.

'What are you supposed to do with this?' Julie asked. She didn't really know what a fondue set was.

'You can cook things in it,' said Henkie, who wasn't too sure either. 'Or you can melt cheese in it.'

'I don't like cheese,' said Julie. 'Why do you always pick such stupid things?'

'For the fun of it,' said Henkie. 'Anyway, it isn't a stupid thing.' He put the pan and the forks back in the box.

'And what are you going to tell your mother when you take that stupid thing home?' asked Julie.

'It isn't stupid,' Henkie said again, but what to do with the stolen goods was indeed becoming more and more of a problem.

Under Henkie's bed there was a box and a rubbish bag full of all kinds of things that had been taken from shops. His mother was sure to find them sooner or later and ask questions about them. What would he do then? He could hardly say that they were all things that he had found out by the dustbins. They all looked brand new. Some of them still had the prices on, too. No, his mother must never set eyes on them.

'Can't you take it home with you?' Henkie asked.

'No, I can't,' said Julie. 'I share a room with my little sister and she tells everyone everything that I do. She even tells them if I just lie down and read. She tells my mother and father everything.'

'You've helped with everything else,' said Henkie. 'Surely you can take this box home and say that you found it out by the dustbin?'

'They always empty the dustbins on Tuesday,' Julie answered, 'and it's Friday today. I don't want that stupid thing anyway.'

'I've got some more sweets here,' said Henkie. 'Cough sweets and some toffees.'

'I wouldn't mind a toffee,' said Julie. As she ate, she said: 'You know, we really ought to find a hiding place somewhere where we can store things.'

'You don't mean we should bury everything, do you?' asked Henkie.

'No, not in the ground,' Julie answered. 'They'd get all dirty and rusty. No, I mean that we need a place where we can keep stuff and where we can use them too. Like that fondue set.'

'Yes, that's a good idea,' said Henkie.

It was half past five and dusk. Lights were going on, shops were closing. A police car drove past them very slowly and so they turned down a side street. They had almost finished the packet of cough sweets.

They saw a black cat and Henkie decided to give him a cough sweet too but the animal darted away.

'I know what,' said Julie. 'Come on, we'll follow that cat.'

The cat set off at a trot and then turned left.

They ran after the animal. The fondue set rattled as they ran. They turned left too.

The cat turned left again and then left again and then left again and they ended up exactly where they had started.

'This is where we were before,' said Henkie.

'I know that,' said Julie. 'Do you think I've lost my marbles or something?'

But still they followed the cat, mainly because Julie wanted to. They turned left again.

'He's going round in circles,' said Henkie. He was getting tired of running.

But just at that moment the cat crossed the street and turned down an alleyway, a passage about one and a half metres wide.

They came at last to an open space, where there were some derelict houses. Rubble was everywhere, and planks of wood and rusty iron bars. Tall plants with prickles were growing all over but the cat knew the way and ran towards a fence near a row of old houses. He stopped and sat down for a moment, as though he were waiting for them, and then he suddenly jumped over the fence and disappeared.

'That's where the cat lives, I think,' said Julie. 'I've seen him round here before.'

'Those houses are empty,' said Henkie. 'They've been boarded up.'

'If that cat can get in, then so can we,' answered Julie.

'We can climb over the fence,' said Henkie.

'I wish I was a cat,' said Julie.

She thought that the fence looked rather high. She may have been nine years old but she was a bit on the small side.

Henkie put down the fondue set and stood with his back to the fence.

'Come and stand on my hands,' he said.

Julie stood on Henkie's hands and was able to look over the fence.

'What can you see?' asked Henkie. He could only see Julie's stomach.

'The cat's gone,' said Julie.

'I didn't ask what you *can't* see,' said Henkie. 'I asked what you *can* see.'

'I can see something you can't see,' said Julie.

'Has it got glass in it?' asked Henkie.

'No, it hasn't any glass. It's a wooden door. It hasn't got a handle either.'

'Is there a window?' asked Henkie.

'Yes, there's a window,' said Julie. 'The glass is broken but there are some planks across it.'

'What else can you see?' Henkie wanted to know.

'Rubbish,' said Julie. 'There's some empty paint tins lying about and a roll of lino. And there's water and there's part of a bed. It's leaning against the fence. It's a thing with bars on it. You could use it as a sort of ladder but it'd have to be on the other side, of course.'

'You're getting too heavy,' said Henkie. 'Get down.'

Julie jumped down and Henkie wiped his fingers on the fence. And that's how he got a splinter in his hand.

'If we lean a piece of wood on this side of the fence, we can use it to climb over,' said Julie. 'That bit of bed is just like a ladder.'

'Let's do it later on,' said Henkie. 'After tea.'

While he was having tea, Henkie asked his mother what a fondue set was.

'It's – it's a pan that you put white wine in to heat it up,' she said as she stirred her cup of tea. 'You melt cheese in it. And then you make a sort of porridge of cornflour, nutmeg and pepper, and then you add a little brandy and you stir it into the melted cheese. It's lovely with chunks of bread.' She made a smacking sound with her lips as if she could actually taste the cheese sauce. 'Why do you want to know, anyway? Don't you like your omelette?'

'I only asked,' said Henkie.

'You don't only ask something like that,' she said.

'Why not?' asked Henkie.

'Because people will think you're stupid.'

'I can ask really difficult questions too, if I want to,' said Henkie. He was getting tired of this conversation already.

'That question about the fondue set wasn't difficult,' said his mother. 'Not if you already know what a fondue set is.'

'What a boring conversation!' Henkie thought.

Serve him right for mentioning the fondue set in the first place.

After his meal of herb omelette and a tub of yoghurt, Henkie dragged the plastic bag from under his bed

80

and told his mother that he had some rubbish to take out.

'Make sure you don't throw it just anywhere in the street,' she said. She was sitting down, looking through a magazine. She was probably hunting for a knitting pattern or a recipe for cheese fondue.

She often looked through magazines, always on the lookout for new knitting patterns, recipes, diets and problems. The melon diet, Why is our dog losing his fur?, How can I tell if my husband is deceiving me?, Jumpers with flowers on, A young skin, Happy knitting, Red cabbage, Chocolate cake, Stuffed eggs, Easter bunnies . . .

It was now well and truly dark outside and fairly quiet too. Most people were either eating, washing up or watching television.

Julie was waiting for Henkie in Little Church Street. He had his flashlight and he shone it on her. Julie had her green mask on and her eyes glittered. She had a hammer with her.

'It's my father's,' she said. 'We'll be able to get the door open with this.' She waved the hammer as if she was breaking down a door.

They saw the cat again by the fence; at least, they saw two little eyes when Henkie shone his flashlight on it.

'Oh, it's you again, is it?' Julie said to the cat. She was very excited at the thought of wearing a mask in the dark and breaking down doors with a hammer.

'Did anyone follow you?' Henkie asked her.

'What do you mean, follow?' asked Julie.

81

'Well, did anyone see you wearing that stupid thing?' Henkie asked, shining his flashlight on Julie once again. It was the red tassel on top that annoyed him most. It looked like a little flame.

'I don't think so,' said Julie. She found a couple of planks and propped them against the fence at the spot where the part of the bed rested on the other side.

'I don't think so, I don't think so . . .' Henkie grumbled as he put the fondue set in the bag with the other things. 'Surely you must know one way or the other. You stick out like a sore thumb in that thing.'

'Give me that,' said Julie. She was sitting on the fence now and put out her hand for the bag.

The bed looked firm enough and it wasn't long before she was standing in a sort of courtyard.

'Watch out, there's water here,' Julie said, and Henkie shone his flashlight on the door.

They didn't need the hammer after all because the door opened without any difficulty. It led into a sort of little kitchen, with a dresser with no doors on it. Some broken flower pots were standing on it. The tiles on the walls were broken and electric wires were hanging loose.

'Perhaps we could leave our things here,' said Henkie, looking for a place for the bag.

The door into the hall had been lifted from its hinges and was leaning against the wall. There was a heap of paper in the hall, mainly old newspapers and advertising leaflets. Somewhere there was a toilet that stank to high heaven.

'There's a sitting room here on the right,' said Julie.

82

They went into the room. A flex hung from the centre of the ceiling and someone had tied an old shoe to the end. There was a chair without a seat and a steel coathanger was hanging from a nail on the wall. There were great piles of paper on the floor here, too.

'The whole place stinks,' said Julie. It seemed that her mask didn't stop her from smelling things.

'It's the cat,' said Henkie. 'And it's damp. There hasn't been any heating here for years.' He shone his flashlight on a rusty cast-iron stove. The damper was open and an old broom-handle was sticking out.

'This place is a real tip,' said Julie.

'Quiet, I can hear something,' Henkie whispered. He switched off his flashlight and they stood in silence. They could hear each other breathing.

'I can't hear anything.' Julie was whispering too. 'I can't hear anything at all. You only said it to scare me.'

'No,' said Henkie. 'I really did hear something. A cough or something.'

'It could have been that cat,' said Julie. 'Perhaps it's got a cold.'

'I've never heard of that before,' said Henkie.

'Never heard of what?' asked Julie.

'A cat with a cough, of course,' answered Henkie. 'I've never heard of that before.' He switched his flashlight on again and shone it on a wall cupboard that had no door. It didn't have any shelves left either.

'Perhaps we could keep our stuff in there,' he said. 'There's a door in the hall that might fit and there are bound to be some planks outside that we can use to make shelves.'

'Perhaps there's a better cupboard upstairs,' said Julie.

They walked into the hall and up the stairs.

'I hope these stairs are strong enough,' said Julie.

'They'll be all right for you,' said Henkie.

'This house has been empty for years,' said Julie. 'The staircase might have rotted away.' She tapped one of the stairs with her hammer.

The stairs were thick with dust and grit, and dense grey cobwebs hung on the walls, like the decorations at some ghastly witches' feast.

'There's still a curtain hanging at this window,' said Julie.

'Leave it alone,' said Henkie. 'We don't want anyone to see us nosing around in here.'

They reached a landing. Some of the floorboards were loose and cracked. The bottom half of the walls was painted dark green and the top half had been plastered white. They were covered with nails and cracks, and there was a patch that looked as though someone had thrown a ripe tomato at it. There were some doors too, and when they pushed open the first one they came to, they were knocked back by the dreadful smell.

A body was lying on an old carpet in the middle of the room. It was lying on its side and Henkie's first thought was that it was a corpse. He tugged Julie's sleeve and pointed with his flashlight.

'There's someone there,' said Henkie. 'A man . . .'

'I can see that for myself,' said Julie. 'I'm not blind, you know.'

Henkie shone his flashlight on the man. He was wearing pointed shoes with worn soles, white socks and a grey overcoat. There was vomit on the carpet near his face.

The man groaned and coughed and opened one eye when Henkie shone the flashlight on his face.

'Hello,' said Henkie.

The man groaned again and closed his eyes. Perhaps he couldn't stand the light.

'Take off that stupid hood,' Henkie grumbled at Julie. 'He'll get angry in a minute, maybe.'

'It isn't a stupid hood,' said Julie, but she took off the mask and stuffed it into her coat pocket. 'He'll know me again now.'

'So what?' said Henkie.

'Anyway, he won't be able to do anything,' said Julie. 'He's sick or drunk.'

She had seen her father when he was drunk more than once. He'd lie on the sofa for hours on end, out for the count.

'I can't see a bottle,' said Henkie, shining his flashlight back and forth.

'Are you ill?' Julie said to the man.

The eye opened again and the eyebrow lifted. The man moved his shoulder and rolled on to his back.

The threadbare carpet on which the man was lying gave Henkie an idea.

'Hey!' he said to Julie. 'I think that he's a foreigner. That's why he doesn't understand us. He doesn't understand Dutch.'

85

By now the man had raised himself a little and was leaning on one arm. He made a movement with the other.

'He wants something,' said Julie.

'He wants a drink,' said Henkie.

'Do you want a drink?' Julie asked the man, and she pretended to empty a cup of something down her throat.

The man nodded and lay down again.

'There you are, he wants something to drink,' said Julie.

'Perhaps he'd like something to eat too,' said Henkie. 'We've still got some toffees left.'

'Perhaps he doesn't want anything,' said Julie. 'He's ill. He may have a fever and you're usually thirsty then.'

'Then we'd better get some water,' said Henkie.

'And something to eat too, perhaps,' said Julie.

'But no one must know what we're doing,' said Henkie.

'No, of course not,' answered Julie. 'They'd only find our store room.'

Henkie knew where to find a sleeping bag at home, in the hall cupboard.

'What on earth are you doing now?' his mother called from the sitting room. 'Why are you coming in and out the whole time?' She was busy with some knitting. 'Have you finished your homework already?'

Henkie said that he had finished his homework. He hadn't really been given any homework at all.

The man in the old house was clearly pleased with the sleeping bag. He took off his jacket and rolled it up to serve as a pillow. Then he took off his shoes and crawled into the bag, clothes and all.

Julie arrived then with rusks, an apple, a carton of milk, a little carton of apple juice with a straw, and a rip in her trousers.

'Look at that!' she said. 'I tore it on that stupid fence.'

'It'll give you something else to sew at school.' Henkie grinned.

'If my mother sees it she'll blow her top,' said Julie. 'I can't stay much longer anyway.'

Henkie gestured to the man that they were leaving and laid his flashlight next to the sleeping bag.

The man put a hand out of the bag and gave a little wave.

When they had climbed over the fence once more, Julie started on again about her torn trousers.

'If my mother finds out she'll give me a really good hiding,' she said.

'Then hit her back,' said Henkie.

'My mother's much stronger than I am, and anyway, she'll call my father and he can really pack a punch,' said Julie.

This was something that Henkie didn't have to worry about. His father had gone away a couple of years ago. He had come back once or twice to collect clothes and furniture but after that Henkie hadn't seen him any more.

'Why don't you cut the legs off?' asked Henkie.

'Then you'd have a pair of shorts. Or you could say that a dog bit you but you don't know which dog it was. Just so long as you don't say that we came here to hide one or two things.'

'I don't really like the idea of leaving those things there,' said Julie.

'Why not?' asked Henkie.

'It isn't a good place, that's all,' said Julie. 'Because that man's there. He could take away the lot.'

'Rubbish,' said Henkie. 'He won't take anything. He's as sick as a dog. Anyway, I put that bag of stuff in the kitchen.'

'That bloke'll be right as rain tomorrow after he's had something to eat and drink,' said Julie. 'And he'll take the lot with him. Including your sleeping bag and the flashlight.'

'I don't like the sound of that,' said Henkie. 'That sleeping bag cost an awful lot. We'll just have to go and take a look first thing tomorrow morning, before school.'

'We haven't got any school tomorrow,' said Julie. 'Tomorrow's Saturday.'

'Even better,' said Henkie. 'Then we'll get up early. We'll go and have a look at seven o'clock.'

'And we'll take some food for him,' said Julie. 'We can boil an egg in the fondue pan.'

'Good idea,' said Henkie. 'We'd better take some butter with us, then.'

'And an egg,' said Julie.

Saturday 7.38 a.m.

'You're late,' said Henkie, stamping his feet on the step because they were cold.

'I didn't sleep very well,' said Julie. She had a bag with her.

'Did you get a good hiding?' asked Henkie.

'No,' said Julie. 'She didn't notice anything. And I've mended my trousers really well. Look!'

Proudly she showed Henkie how beautifully the rip had been mended.

'It took an awfully long time,' said Julie. 'I didn't want my little sister to see so I had to do it in the dark and after a bit I found that I'd sewn my trousers to the sheet.'

Henkie laughed again. 'And then?'

'Then I had to unpick it all. After that I went and sat in the toilet. At least I could have the light on in there. Have you got any food?'

'Yes,' Henkie answered. 'I've got an egg in here.' He slapped the breast pocket of his jacket. 'Oh no! It's broken!'

Now it was Julie's turn to laugh.

'I've got milk, sandwiches and butter,' she said.

'Give me a sandwich, will you?' said Henkie. 'I haven't had anything to eat yet.'

Julie produced a plastic bag of sandwiches. She gave one to Henkie and ate one herself as well.

'Now I've only got two left,' she said. 'But I brought an apple with me too.'

They climbed over the fence once more, and Julie was extra careful this time so that she wouldn't rip her trousers again. Henkie helped her with the bag of food but it wasn't really necessary.

The man was still lying on the carpet and he had hardly touched anything. Perhaps he had drunk a little apple juice. The straw was in the carton, anyway.

He was groaning and sweating terribly.

'He's in a very bad way,' said Henkie.

'He's as sick as anything,' said Julie.

'He's got a piece of paper in his hand,' said Henkie.

Henkie took an old brown envelope from the man's hand. One word had been written on it with a blunt pencil:

Medecin

'He's ill,' said Henkie. 'He wants medicine.'

'It isn't as simple as that,' said Julie. 'What kind of medicine does he want?'

'Aspirin, maybe,' said Henkie.

'Or maybe not,' said Julie. 'He could get even more ill if he takes the wrong medicine, or he might even die . . .'

'But he might die anyway if we don't fetch any

medicine at all,' said Henkie. 'And it would be our fault . . .'

'I know!' Julie said, after a moment's thought. 'We'll go to Jan-Willem.'

'Who's Jan-Willem?' asked Henkie.

'Jan-Willem lives down our street,' said Julie. 'He works in the hospital and he knows a lot about illness. He told me once how you give injections and how you draw off people's blood.'

'But he'll give the whole game away!' Henkie wailed.

'We'll ask him not to tell,' said Julie. 'And we just won't say anything at all about the things we've taken from shops.'

There was nothing else for it. They couldn't just leave the strange man lying in the house. He might die and they might get the blame . . .

They rang Jan-Willem's doorbell.

They rang again.

'He's out,' said Henkie.

'No, he isn't,' said Julie. 'His car's there.'

She pressed the bell once more.

After a while Jan-Willem opened the door. He looked very sleepy, his hair was standing on end. He was wearing a maroon dressing gown. 'Where's the fire?' he asked, and yawned. 'Come on in, it's blooming cold.'

Inside the curtains were drawn.

'Careful,' said Jan-Willem. 'There are records on the floor.' He opened the curtains and there were indeed a lot of records scattered over the floor. David

Bowie, Culture Club, Pink Floyd, Climax Blues Band. On the wall there was an enormous poster of some desert or other with a line of footprints in the sand.

'We've got a problem,' said Julie.

'But you've got to keep quiet about it,' said Henkie.

'I'm not saying anything,' said Jan-Willem.

'We were in an old house,' said Julie. 'One of those derelict houses over there . . .' She waved her hand. 'There's a man inside and he's very ill.'

'He's been sick,' Henkie added. 'And he won't eat anything. And he had this note.'

Henkie handed Jan-Willem the envelope with the word 'Medecin' on it.

'If you ask me, "medecin" means doctor,' said Jan-Willem. 'But I'm not a doctor.'

'He seems like a foreigner to me,' said Henkie.

'And he's very ill,' said Julie. 'He's sweating **and** groaning and his breath smells.'

Jan-Willem thought for a moment, scratching his chest through his dressing gown.

'The best thing we can do is phone the police,' he said after a while.

'But you said you wouldn't give the game away!' Julie shouted. 'You promised not to tell! If you warn the police then they'll want to know what we were doing there.'

'And exactly what *were* you doing in an empty house so early in the morning?' asked Jan-Willem.

'Nothing,' said Henkie. 'We were curious, that's all, and so we just went into the house.'

'We were chasing a cat,' said Julie, 'and I tore my trousers. And then we heard a cough and then we found the man in a room upstairs. We took him something to eat but he didn't want anything. He really looks awfully sick. And that's why we thought of you because you work at the hospital.'

'I've got the day off,' said Jan-Willem. 'I worked all last night. I'm still in bed.'

'But we can't leave that man lying there,' said Henkie. 'He could die at any moment and then they'll find our fingerprints.'

'O.K.,' said Jan-Willem. 'I'll come and have a look in a little while. I'll just get dressed. Put on some coffee for me. Everything's ready in the kitchen. You just need to press the switch.'

Henkie and Julie went into the kitchen and everything was indeed ready: a whole week's washing up and a coffee percolator. Julie pressed the switch.

'You can do some of that washing up, if you want!' Jan-Willem called out. 'Or tidy up these records.' He had put a record on: a piece of music in which piano notes were joined by guitars and trumpets to make a sort of stew with here and there a slice of guitar and a morsel of piano.

Jan-Willem listened to the music as he put on his socks and shoes and stirred his cup of coffee as if he was searching for something in it. When the record was finished, he said that he would go and look now.

'We'll show you the way,' said Julie as they set off.

At the fence Jan-Willem said, 'I'll go and take a look by myself. You two stay here.'

And he climbed over the fence.

'Don't rip your trousers,' said Julie.

They stayed where they were, watching the cat stalk birds in the gutter. Henkie threw a stone in the direction of the cat.

'Don't do that!' Julie shouted. 'You big bully!'

'I'm helping the birds,' said Henkie.

Then Jan-Willem was back again.

'That man can't stay there,' he said. 'He's really very ill.'

'What's wrong with him?' Henkie asked.

'I don't know,' said Jan-Willem. 'It could be anything. He's got a high fever anyway. He needs to have a thorough examination. It would be best if he went into hospital right away. You two go home and I'll arrange something.'

'As long as you don't tell anyone we were here,' said Henkie.

'That's why you must go home now before anyone notices you. Come and see me this afternoon and I'll let you know what happened. I'll think of some story or other.'


A few days later, Henkie Visser and Julie Snoep were walking round the hospital. They had lost their way and they didn't really know where they were supposed to go.

'We'd better ask someone where he is,' said Julie.

'It's out of visiting hours,' said Henkie.

They had just walked in through a back entrance and gone up in the lift to the first floor it stopped at.

A couple of nurses were sitting in a glass cage, eating cakes. They were eating chocolate éclairs and cream slices with cherries as red as their lips. One of the nurses came out of the cage.

'I expect you'd like a cake, too, wouldn't you?'

'You bet,' said Julie.

'That's what I thought,' said the nurse. She licked her thumb. Her nails were as red as her lips. Her tongue was pink and she just stood there, staring at them.

'We're looking for someone,' said Henkie, 'but we don't know where he is.'

'Is it a man or a woman?'

'A man,' said Julie.

'Then you're in the wrong place,' said the nurse. 'It's women and babies only on this side. The men are right on the other side. Straight on and turn right.' She waved her hand as if she was throwing a tennis ball.

'Straight on and turn right,' repeated Julie.

They passed some more glass. Behind it were glass cots with babies sleeping inside them.

'Little sleeping beauties,' said Henkie.

They came upon women in overalls, trolleys of food and someone with his head in a bandage. You could only see his eyes.

'It looks just like your mask,' said Henkie.

'Straight on,' said Julie.

Men in pyjamas sat smoking and coughing in a room. One of them was tearing something out of a newspaper. The television was on but it was only showing the test card. Someone was walking up and down on crutches. There was no one there who

95

looked like the man they were searching for.

They couldn't find him in any of the other rooms either.

'We'd better ask someone,' said Julie. 'We can hardly look in every single bed.'

But they still managed to walk past a great many beds before someone said: 'Hey, what are you children doing here?'

It was a tall man with a white coat and some cards in his hand.

They explained who they were looking for.

'Are you relatives of this man?' the man asked.

'No, doctor,' said Julie.

'I'm not a doctor,' the man said. But he didn't say who he really was either.

'I know exactly who you're looking for,' said the man with the cards, which just had little squares and figures on them. 'We're looking for him too, as it happens. He disappeared suddenly yesterday evening or during the night.'

'What do you mean?' asked Henkie.

'He walked out of the hospital without anyone noticing. He was scared.'

'Was he going to have an operation?' Julie asked.

'No, not that,' said the man, putting the cards in his pocket. 'He was scared of the police.'

'Was he a thief?' Henkie asked.

'No, he wasn't,' said the man, taking a ballpoint pen from another pocket. 'He was just a foreigner without any papers.'

'Do you need papers in a hospital then?' Henkie asked.

96

'Yes, you do, really,' said the man, putting the ballpoint pen in his breast pocket. 'And you certainly need them outside. If the police find out that he hasn't any papers then he'll have to go back to his own country.'

'Where has he gone now?' Julie asked.

'That we don't know,' said the man, buttoning his white coat. 'He just went off in his pyjamas with a coat on top. And the silly thing about it is that he isn't even better yet.'

'He must have been really scared of the police, then,' said Henkie.

When they walked out of the hospital a little later, Julie produced an orange from her jacket pocket.

'We can eat this ourselves, now,' Julie said.

'Where did you get that from?' Henkie asked.

'Aha!' said Julie.

# The shelter

Hardly anyone ever came to the waste ground by the old laundry. It was covered with tall dry grass, rust-brown plants with lots of little round seeds, and shoulder-high balsams with small pink flowers. But there was also a round bare patch and that was were Matthew and Vonnie were digging.

They dug black sand away at first, and then grey, pale yellow, white and orange sand. That was a bit damp.

'This is lovely sand!' said Vonnie.

'We've got to go deeper,' said Matthew. 'We've got to be able to sit in it easily.'

They weren't the only people on the waste ground. Bennie Bogaerts was sitting among the balsam plants. He had seen that they were digging and was curious to know what was going on.

It seemed very hard work, digging. Matthew was sweating and he rubbed his face with his hand. It left black marks.

'The deeper the better,' said Vonnie.

'Yes, it must be really deep,' said Matthew, 'but water mustn't get in it. And there must be planks round the sides. To keep the radiation out.'

'And we'll lay planks and bits of plastic and sand on the roof,' said Vonnie. 'Then we can grow plants and grass on top. Because no one must be able to see it. It must be a secret . . .'

'What must be a secret?' asked Bennie, who had crept stealthily closer and overheard the last few words.

'Oh no, it's Bennie Bogaerts,' said Vonnie. 'He's found out everything now.'

But she carried on digging just the same.

'What are you two doing?' Bennie asked.

'What does it look like?' said Matthew. He piled a heap of sand on Bennie's feet. 'We're digging.'

'Yes, I can see that,' said Bennie, kicking some sand back in the hole. 'Are you looking for treasure?'

'No,' said Vonnie. 'We're just digging, that's all.'

'Can I dig too?' asked Bennie.

'Well, all right then,' said Matthew. 'But you'd better not tell anyone what we're doing here. It's got to stay a secret, a deep, deep secret.'

Bennie Bogaerts jumped into the hole and began to scoop sand away from the sides with his hands. He dug a sort of cave.

'You mustn't dig a cave,' said Matthew. 'The sides must be nice and straight because we're going to lay planks across after a while.'

'I knew it!' said Bennie. 'You *are* making something! You're digging a hideout or something like that!'

'No,' said Matthew. 'We're not making a secret hideout. We're making a shelter.'

'For when war comes,' said Vonnie.

'For when nuclear war comes,' Matthew explained. 'Then at least we'll have a place to sit in.'

'You've got to sit in the ground,' Vonnie went on, 'because when one of those missiles drops, then all the houses fall flat — wham!' She made a chopping movement with her hand.

'Everything'll be knocked down,' Matthew added. 'All those houses there and the lamp-posts, and that tall chimney by the laundry.'

'Well, that won't be so bad,' said Bennie. 'It isn't used any more. It'll fall down all by itself one of these days. Look how far it's leaning over already.'

'There's a flash of light first of all and then everything gets burned up,' said Matthew. 'The trees are turned straight into charcoal. The windows in the houses are smashed. And the tarmac on the roads goes all soft and starts to bubble.'

'And the people who aren't in shelters get their skin burnt,' said Vonnie. 'And their eyes pop out.'

'Hey, what do you mean, their eyes pop out?' asked Bennie, with a shudder.

'Well, they just sort of melt,' said Matthew. 'That's what happened before.'

'In Japan,' said Vonnie. 'When they dropped the atom bomb. Everything burst into flames. And those were only very small bombs.'

'The missiles they've got now are much worse,' said Matthew. 'They're a lot bigger, as big as that chimney over there.'

They all stared for a moment at the laundry chimney. It looked very crooked and sad.

'It's a good thing you're making a shelter, and I can help too,' said Bennie.

'Then you'd better make the sides straight,' said Matthew.

'He can go and look for planks of wood,' said Vonnie. 'There are some over by the laundry.'

And Bennie went to fetch the planks from the laundry right away. He dragged them through the grass to the shelter. He also found an old zinc bucket without a bottom, and there was a concrete drainpipe too but he couldn't lift that.

'Well done,' said Matthew. 'Those are good planks.'

'There's a big pipe too,' said Bennie. 'But I couldn't bring it with me.'

'We can use just about anything,' said Matthew. 'Iron and wood and stone, everything. And there should really be lead on the roof . . .'

'That's much too heavy, surely?' said Vonnie. 'The roof would fall in. It'd be better to use planks and put plastic over them.'

'Plastic won't keep the radiation out,' said Matthew. 'Radiation's really awful. It strikes you dead just like that and it poisons everything.'

'Perhaps we could still put planks and plastic and sand on the roof anyway,' said Vonnie. 'Perhaps it might help just a bit.'

It grew into a small shelter, a sort of dark cave with an old carpet that closed the entrance from the inside.

A couple of people could sit inside it with their knees drawn up. The roof was low, and sand fell down if you bumped your head against it. Sometimes sand fell down if you didn't bump your head.

'We can block up cracks with newspapers,' said Vonnie.

'Yes, we'd better block them up,' said Matthew. 'We don't want sand falling on us when we go to sleep.'

'And we don't want it falling in the food either,' said Bennie, who was feeling hungry. He had been working very hard. He had found plastic bags, he had sawn and hammered and hit his finger. He licked the painful finger but it didn't stop him from feeling hungry.

'Yes, we've got to have food,' said Matthew. 'We must keep it here and put it in bottles and pots.'

'That'll be best,' said Vonnie. 'Then sand won't get in it. And we can fetch a bottle of water.'

'We'll make a store,' said Matthew. 'The food in the shops and houses won't be any good after an explosion. The radiation gets everywhere and if you eat bread or anything like that, your hair and teeth fall out . . .'

'We must have sticking plaster, too,' said Vonnie. 'And iodine and bandages.'

'I've got a sore finger,' said Bennie.

'We'll put a shelf up here,' said Matthew. 'The food can go on it and a medicine chest. Come on, let's go and find things.'

They went to find things and, despite his sore finger, Bennie fixed a shelf to the side of the shelter.

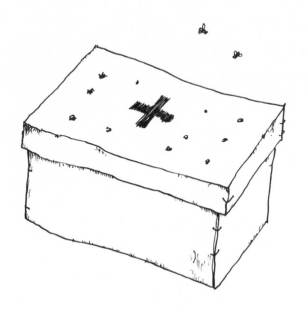

Matthew brought some apples and a shoe box on which he had drawn a red cross with a felt-tip pen. Inside it were a bag of humbugs, a tin of stewed tomatoes and a couple of onions. He arranged everything on the shelf.

Vonnie came back leading her three-year-old sister by the hand. The little girl had a lollipop in her mouth and so had Vonnie.

Matthew said: 'What have you brought?'

'This is my little sister,' said Vonnie. 'I've got **to** look after her.'

'When the war really comes, we can eat her,' said Bennie. 'She's nice and fat.' He gave the child's plump little arm a gentle pinch.

'She can come in with us,' Vonnie decided. 'She's only little.'

'Then I'll fetch my little brother too,' said Bennie. 'He's even smaller. He's still in a playpen.'

'There's definitely no room for a playpen,' said Matthew. 'There isn't room for everyone. That goes without saying. There's no room for grown-ups, for instance. The roof is too low for them.'

'They'll have to build their own shelters,' said Bennie.

'They've already got them,' said Matthew, 'but they won't let just anyone in them. Crooks aren't allowed in.'

'And soldiers aren't either,' said Bennie, 'because they've got to fight and shoot off the missiles. No, not everyone's allowed in.'

'How do they decide then?' Vonnie asked.

'Maybe they draw lots,' said Matthew. 'Or perhaps they don't allow old people in and perhaps there has to be the same number of women as there are men.'

'It's the same with us,' said Vonnie.

'Only if you count your little sister as a woman,' said Bennie.

'And what about the animals?' asked Vonnie.

'All the animals will be dead after an explosion like that,' said Matthew.

105

'Except the animals who live in holes,' said Bennie. 'Or in the sea.'

'Perhaps we could take some animals into our shelter,' said Vonnie.

'One elephant and the hole will be full,' grinned Bennie.

'We could take small animals,' said Vonnie. 'A spider, a little bird and a mouse.'

'Two of each, you mean,' said Matthew. 'Like Noah.'

'Who's Noah?' asked Bennie.

'He's the man in the Bible who set off in a big boat with a whole lot of animals,' said Vonnie. 'And it rained for forty days and there was a big flood and in the ark there were all kinds of animals. Two of each sort.'

'That's right,' said Matthew. 'Noah was in the ark and he had two of each kind of animal with him: two horses, two cows, two pigs, two giraffes . . .'

'Giraffes won't fit in,' said Bennie, 'and cows won't either.'

'Boo!' said Vonnie's little sister. It sounded rather strange because she kept the lollipop in her mouth the whole time.

'We'll find little animals,' said Vonnie. 'Two spiders, two flies, two beetles . . .'

'You'll have to catch more flies than that because the spiders will need food. And the flies, what will *they* eat?'

'We'll give them a bit of lollipop,' said Vonnie. 'That'll keep them going for a long time.'

They went to look for animals.

106

First they tried to catch spiders. In a corner of the laundry a fat spider was sitting in a tangle of threads.

'Come on, out with you!' Bennie commanded, and he jabbed the creature with a blade of grass.

The spider ran off a little way and then suddenly stopped dead on the wall. Bennie quickly put a jam jar over it.

'Gotcher!' said Matthew. 'Oh look, one of his leg's come off.'

'That doesn't matter,' said Bennie. 'He's got eight altogether.' He carefully slid the lid on the jar.

'Now for another one,' said Vonnie.

'You can't put two spiders together just like that,' said Bennie. 'They'll eat each other up.'

There were woodlice under the concrete drainpipe and a centipede that moved very quickly but was caught just the same.

They put everything that they found in the shoe-box with the red cross on it. Vonnie had caught a grasshopper and they could hear it crashing against the sides of the box.

'Perhaps they'll all eat each other up,' said Bennie.

'Grasshoppers eat grass,' Vonnie told him. She picked a bunch of grass and pushed it carefully inside the box. And she pushed some sand inside too and a stone for the woodlice to creep beneath.

Vonnie wrote down all they found on a piece of paper. She ended up with the following list of animals:

1 grasshopper

1 ladybird

4 ants

2 beetles

1 earwig

2 woodlice

1 centipede

1 worm

1 funny animal
with feelers

1 long black
wriggly thing

1 spider

2 pink slugs

'Those four ants won't be much use,' said Bennie. 'You really need the queen but it's anyone's guess where she is, deep under the ground somewhere.'

'So she's got her own underground shelter,' said Vonnie.

'What a business it all is!' said Matthew, who had been trying to catch bees by the balsam plants. He had tried to catch a sparrow too but it had flown away, of course. 'How did Noah manage?' he wanted to know. 'How did Noah catch all those animals?'

When you began to think about it, it really was a marvellous story.

'Did Noah have any fleas in the ark?' Matthew asked.

'Of course,' answered Vonnie. 'Otherwise we wouldn't have any fleas now. And perhaps he didn't really need to catch any of those anyway.'

'Why not?' asked Matthew.

'Perhaps he already had them!' Vonnie laughed.

'And did he have woodworm in the ark? And wasps?' asked Matthew.

'He had everything,' said Vonnie. 'In cages and cases, in pens and boxes.'

'Surely *we* aren't going to collect everything?' asked Bennie. 'I don't really want any wasps and midges and things in our shelter.'

They were all agreed on that. All the stinging creatures would be left outside.

'But we really do need a dove,' said Matthew.

'Why a dove?' asked Bennie.

'Don't you really know the story of Noah's ark?' asked Matthew.

'No,' said Bennie Bogaerts.

'When it stopped raining, Noah made a hole in the roof of the ark and let a dove fly out through it. And the dove came back later on with a green branch. And Noah could tell from this that everything was all right and that trees were growing again. Have you seen a dove anywhere?'

'Surely we don't have to follow exactly everything that Noah did in the story?' said Bennie.

'No, not exactly,' said Matthew. 'But it *would* be nice, wouldn't it?'

'We've got a zebra finch at home,' said Bennie.

'Well, go and fetch it then!' shouted Matthew.

A little later Bennie came running back with the zebra finch. It was a beautiful little bird with orange specks on his cheeks and a red beak. He peered at the children timidly with his head on one side.

'Come on,' said Matthew. 'Let's pretend that a missile is about to come down.'

They crept into the hole and pulled the carpet across the entrance. It was dark and they sat huddled together. Vonnie had her little sister on her lap and Bennie was clutching the little bird.

'A missile is going to explode any minute now,' said Matthew. 'We'll all be very scared and so we'll stay in the shelter for a while. Then we'll let the bird fly away and if he comes back then we'll know that everything is safe and there aren't any more missiles. Quiet now, I'm going to start the countdown . . .'

They were all very quiet and there wasn't a peep from the little bird either.

'Ten,' said Matthew. 'Nine. That's what they do with missiles. Eight. Seven. Six. Five. Four. Three. Two. *One*. BOOM!' He shouted the last word very loudly. So loudly that Vonnie's little sister began to cry.

'I want my mummy!' she cried. 'I want my mummy! I want my mummy!' It seemed as if she would never stop.

'Keep quiet,' said Vonnie. 'It isn't the real missile.'

'That sounds exactly right, her crying,' said Matthew. 'It's exactly what happens in a war. Now for the bird, hand it over.' He took the bird from Bennie and let it fly away.

'But I'll lose my bird!' Bennie protested.

'What on earth are you all doing?' a voice suddenly asked. It was Vonnie's mother. She lifted the carpet aside. 'Why is that child crying? Come out of that hole at once!'

'It isn't a hole,' said Matthew. 'It's a nuclear shelter.'

But they crawled out of the hole just the same. Vonnie and her little sister had to go home for tea. And Bennie and Matthew too, probably.

Outside the sun was shining as usual, and the zebra finch was sitting on the laundry roof. But even though Bennie called and called, the little bird didn't come back.

'I *knew* we should have had a dove,' said Matthew.

# Unknown soldier

On an afternoon that is filled with sun, a wasp stings my brother's leg. He screams that he is going to die but he dances about just the same.

He is six and I am three.

Later on we see that a wasp has fallen in our tin of treacle. He is lying still and there is a thin splinter on the end of his yellow-black abdomen.

'**That**'s what he stung me with,' says my brother. 'That's what the nasty thing stuck in my leg.' He points to a rag tied around his calf.

He jabs the wasp with a spoon and its head sinks beneath the treacle.

'Serves him right,' says my brother.

It is September 1944. We are living in a village in the south of Holland with a market square with tall trees and a church tower that is even taller than the trees, and with sandy paths that go to the moor or the woods. If you drag your feet, you make clouds of dust and your feet are black in the evening.

One day I am walking along one of the paths. I am going down a cart track and a brown hare jumps out ahead of me. He looks very strange when he runs, as if he's got his hands in his pockets.

He stops every now and then to look back at me, but when I move closer he hops a little further on.

I go past the water mill that always scares me and come to the pool where waterlilies are floating. Dragonflies shoot across the surface like little aeroplanes.

In the water I can see fish that are coloured silver, black and red. They are lying on the bottom, hardly moving at all.

I do not know where the hare has gone.

One day silver slivers fall from the sky. On one side they are silver and on the other they seem to be black. They are coiled like a girl's ringlets. We dance in this strange rain, and Ansje from next door keeps jump-

ing up to snatch the slivers from the air.

'They throw them out of aeroplanes,' my brother says. 'That's what the Tommies do.'

The Tommies are fighting the Germans. Everyone knows that, and we are against the Germans. Whenever my mother gives us a peeled carrot, we hold it high in the air and march round singing: 'Orange for ever!', because orange is our national colour.

We are playing in front of the house with our

spades. There are a couple of lime trees and under them some grey sand.

A German car comes driving past. The roof is down. A man is sitting behind the wheel and a lady in a flowered dress is sitting in the back. She is leaning back and laughing, letting her hair blow free.

My brother throws a spadeful of sand at the car and a cloud of dust blows on to the lady.

The car stops a little further on. The lady isn't laughing any more. She is running a hand through her hair and pointing at us with the other.

The man gets angrily out of the car to grab my brother. But he can run very fast and he hides indoors, behind the curtains.


Sometimes there are thunderstorms, at other times there is the sound of rumbling gunfire or else there is bombing.

There is more and more bombing and shelling, and my brother and I often have to go and sit under the table. My mother props mattresses against the sides of the table so that we are sitting in a sort of dark and warm little house.

Sometimes there is a lot of noise. Then you can hear the continuous droning of aeroplanes and sometimes the ground trembles; there are heavy rumbling noises and the sound of whistling and crashing.

My mother walks round and round the table, praying, and she screams when the windows break and shrapnel flies inside.

My father isn't with us. We don't know where he is. He's been gone a long time.

Sometimes we have to get into bed with Mother. It is very cramped.

'They're coming closer all the time,' she says.

The window trembles and so does she.

The man next door and his son Piet are digging a deep hole in the lawn next to our house. Beautifully coloured sand comes out of the hole. They lower into it the concrete circle of the water butt. It lies on its side and they cover the hole with planks of wood and branches.

It has become a hole you can sit in. Planks have been set against the walls and a couple of benches have been made.

'That isn't thunder you can hear,' my brother says to me. He knows that I am scared of thunderstorms. 'Those are guns and tanks and they're shooting everything to pieces. That's why they've made that hole. We can get inside, and all the bullets will fly over our heads.'

And we do have to get into the hole. A lot of people have to get inside: the man and woman next door with their five children, and the three of us. We sit huddled together, and it is dark and warm. An old carpet with holes in it is hanging across the entrance.

There is more and more noise. War is lots of noise. There is a heavy rumbling sound outside and tiles clatter from the rooftops. You can hear the sound of breaking glass, and the whistle and thud of walls collapsing.

116

'Our house . . .' my mother says. Her eyes are wide open, but it is best to keep your eyes closed because sand is falling all the time through the branches above our heads.

And you're supposed to keep your eyes closed when you're praying.

My mother and the lady next door are praying the loudest: 'Hail Mary . . .pray for us sinners, now and at the hour of our death. Amen.'

In the end the praying changes to screaming and crying, and the women want to get out of the hole.

The man next door thinks that it would be best to wait but the women are scared that they'll have to stay in the hole all night and they can't bear the thought of that.

Someone pushes a blanket into my arms and we crawl out of the hole.

Outside it is night.

'Run, Wim. Run, lad!' my mother shouts.

She is carrying little Adje from next door who is still only a baby. She has rolled him in a swanskin blanket and she runs head down past the houses. I try to follow her but it isn't easy with a blanket I keep tripping over. 'Run, lad! Run . . .'

We run into the village.

Why are we doing that? Things are on fire there. Fire is coming from a factory chimney, orange flames are licking the windows of houses.

And the noise.

There is a bandstand in the market square. Under the floor you can reach an enclosed space down a flight of steps. Even more people are sitting there. They have oil lamps with them.

We sit down on the ground. Baby Adje is crying terribly. My mother has been carrying him upside-down by mistake.

Someone has a big pan of gruel that has been boiled in water with little apples. We are all glad to have some of it.

Two German soldiers come down the steps. They have to bend double or else they will bump their dark helmets on the ceiling. They are holding rifles in front of their chests. They are tired and they are sweating. We give them some of our watery gruel.

'They want to protect us,' Mother says.

They go up the steps and fire their guns outside. Later on one of them is dead and the other has gone. My mother won't let me look.

Something wet trickles down the steps. I think it's milk but my brother says: 'That isn't milk. It's blood.'

He is six and I am still only three.

Suddenly a lot starts to happen, there under the bandstand. A line of men comes in. They have to keep their hands on their heads. They are accompanied by soldiers who look quite different from the Germans.

'Yanks,' says my brother, and we look at the short rifles they're carrying. They are weapons with a steel guard instead of a wooden butt.

The space where we're sitting is ideal for guarding prisoners: there is only one way out. But we have to leave. My mother doesn't know where to go because our house has disappeared.

'Come on, we'll find something,' my mother says as she takes us by the hand and helps us up the steps.

It is dark outside but the sky is full of stars. A lot of vehicles with caterpillar tracks are driving across the market square, and heavy lorries and motorbikes. There is a great deal going on and a lot of running to and fro.

When you are three years old you are only little and very close to the ground. You have a good view of things that are lying in the street. And when you are little it isn't easy to step over loose paving stones in the dark. It's just as well that you have your mother's arm to cling on to from time to time.

But I don't only see the paving stones that have been loosened by tanks. I can see something else. A man is lying there; his face is dirty, his mouth is open and his teeth are gleaming.

I have often asked myself since why he was lying there and why he was screaming without making a sound. Was he a German or an American or no one in particular? And what was he doing in the village of trees and sandy paths? Was he dead or was he simply taking a breather?

The memory is clear and hazy at the same time. His face is distinct only for a moment, but his body is grey, dark, no more than a speck in my memory.

# Advertisement

On Saturday the eighteenth of May this year, the following advertisement appeared in a newspaper:

> WE MARC 10 LOES 9 AND MARJORIE 3 ARE LOOKING FOR A FATHER FOR US AND A HUSBAND FOR OUR MOTHER 31 AND SLIM. COLOUR OF SKIN UNIMPORTANT.

On the afternoon of the thirty-first of May, at one minute past four, there was a ring at the doorbell.

'He's one minute late,' said Marc, tapping his watch.

'Check!' said Loes. She had a piece of cardboard to which she had fastened a sheet of paper with a clothes-peg. It had been agreed that she would write everything down. She could write very nicely and quite quickly too, even though she wasn't given detention very often.

'I can see something,' said Marjorie. If she stood on tip-toe she could just see through the letter-box.

'What?' asked Loes, who was curious too.

'Grey legs,' said Marjorie.

A tall man in a grey suit was standing on the step. He had a bunch of yellow flowers in his hand.

Marc, who had thought up the plan almost entirely on his own, looked at the man in silence. He had made up his mind to say, 'Two pints, please,' as if he'd been expecting the milkman. But now that the moment had come he couldn't say anything at all.

'Hello, good afternoon,' said the man.

'He's black . . .' Loes whispered, covering her mouth with the piece of cardboard. She forgot to write anything down for quite a long time.

'You must be Marc, of course,' said the man, pointing to Marc. 'And you're Marloes.'

'Loes,' said Loes, even though she thought that Marloes sounded really special. 'And Marjorie's behind the door.'

The letter-box snapped shut.

'And you must be Mr Emil,' said Marc. 'Come in.'

'My name's really Emil de Wit,' said Emil. 'But I prefer people to call me Emil. Are you surprised that I am black?'

'No, no,' said Marc. 'We said in the advertisement that colour of skin was unimportant.'

'We nearly put colour of shin,' said Loes, who had typed out the advertisement on a piece of paper.

'And now, where's your mother?' asked Emil. 'I've brought her a bunch of flowers. I hope that she likes yellow flowers.' He showed them the bouquet.

It was more like a bush than a bunch, Loes thought. She also thought that yellow suited the man, and anyway she liked yellow flowers herself.

'She isn't home yet,' said Loes. 'But I'll put the flowers in a vase.'

'She's still at work,' said Marc. 'She usually comes home between five and half past. We wanted to meet you first.'

'Come on in,' said Loes, who had taken the bunch of flowers. 'Come into the sitting room.'

The man followed them inside.

'Well, this is the sitting room,' said Marc. 'There are all sorts of things in here.'

Marc was a keen television fan and he headed straight for the television set. 'This is the telly,' he said and turned the knob. 'But there's nothing much on at the moment.'

'And this is the lamp,' said Loes, switching a standard lamp on and off.

'And Monique usually sits here,' said Marc, patting a flowered chair. On the arm of the chair lay a book with a gun, blood and playing cards on the cover.

122

'My mother reads a lot,' he said.

The standard lamp went on and off a couple of times because Marjorie knew how it worked too.

'Do sit down,' said Marc, 'and we'll make some coffee.'

The children ran into the kitchen, leaving the man in the sitting room.

'How many cups will he drink?' Marc asked as he got the percolator ready and took the tin of coffee out of the dresser cupboard.

'I've no idea,' said Loes. 'He's very big, though. He's sure to want two or three cups.'

'Perhaps he doesn't like coffee,' said Marc. 'Perhaps he'd rather have tea.'

'Black men always drink coffee,' said Loes. 'Black coffee with no milk.'

'Go and see what he's doing,' said Marc.

'Do it yourself,' answered Loes, but she went to have a quiet look.

'He's a bit nervous, I expect,' said Marc. 'But at least he isn't a thief.'

Loes was taken aback. It had never crossed her mind. Just imagine if he'd taken something nice or if he was a crook with a knife . . . She went hot all over at the thought.

'Have you got the tray ready?' Marc asked.

Loes found the tray that she liked most of all: it was black with red and blue flowers on it. She put a saucer on it and a cup.

'Make sure it's clean,' said Marc. 'And put some biscuits on a plate. There are some in the cupboard. But don't take the chocolate biscuits.'

'Why not?' asked Loes. 'They're really nice.'

She put four biscuits on a little plate. Soon there were only three because Marjorie could reach them.

'Biscuit,' she said.

'Stop it,' said Loes. 'They're for the man.' And she pulled the biscuit from Marjorie's hand.

The biscuit broke into little pieces and Marjorie started to cry.

'Ssh!' said Marc. 'Stop crying now. The man'll hear you.'

But Marjorie would only stop when she was given another biscuit.

When the coffee percolator began to bubble, they took the tray into the sitting room.

'The coffee's nearly ready,' said Loes.

After that no one knew what to say. They listened to the coffee percolator growling and roaring like an old steam boat.

'Shall I put a record on?' asked Marc. He didn't care for the silence at all. 'We've got hardly any jazz.'

'Put on anything you like,' said Emil. 'It doesn't have to be jazz.'

Marc looked through the records for a while but he couldn't decide. 'Will you do it?' he said to Loes. 'I'll go and have a look at the coffee.'

In the kitchen he looked at the coffee percolator and ate a biscuit. It said San Franciscos on the packet. Loes came into the kitchen with the bunch of flowers. 'You're eating biscuits,' she said.

'Me too,' said Marjorie, who had wandered in after Loes.

Marc took the coffee pot into the sitting room.

'Lovely,' said Emil. 'They didn't have any coffee on the train. Someone usually comes round with a trolley. Have you got any milk?'

'Sorry,' said Marc and he rushed into the kitchen. 'Put those flowers down,' he said to Loes, 'and pour some milk into a jug.'

'Oh, I thought . . .' said Loes.

Together they brought in some milk and sugar for Emil and they gave Marjorie another biscuit to keep her quiet. After that they watched the man on the settee. They watched him drink coffee and eat a San Francisco.

Emil smiled and asked: 'Aren't you having anything?'

'No,' said Loes. 'We're just watching.'

'So I see,' said Emil. He laughed. 'Take a good look.'

'And we want to ask you something,' said Marc.

'And we'll write it all down,' said Loes, picking up her piece of cardboard again.

'Ask away,' said Emil. He put down the coffee cup and folded his arms.

'We know that your name is Emil de Wit,' said Loes. 'And we know how old you are and your address too. It's on this piece of paper.'

'Yes, I wrote all that down,' said Emil.

'But now we want to find out if you're really suitable,' said Marc.

The standard lamp went on and off a couple of times. Marjorie had found the switch again.

'We want to know,' said Loes, 'if you ever hit children.'

125

'What sort of a question is that?' Emil asked.

'Well,' said Marc, 'we had a father once and he hit us sometimes.'

'And hard too!' said Loes. 'Once we were lying in our bedroom talking and he came storming upstairs to hit us. Luckily we just had time to stuff some books into our pyjamas . . .'

'And he hit our mother too,' said Marc.

'And we don't want any more of that,' said Loes.

'It's a long time since I fought anyone,' answered Emil. 'Not since I was at primary school.'

'Wrestling's all right,' Marc decided.

'And playing games, that's all right too,' said Loes. 'Memory or Hare and Tortoise.'

'Marjorie?' asked Marjorie, who thought she'd heard her name.

'Hare and Tortoise?' asked Emil. 'What sort of a game is that?'

'You have to eat lettuce and carrots,' said Loes. 'It's here under the settee.'

'It's not supposed to be there,' said Marc.

Loes dragged the game from under the settee.

'We're not going to play it,' said Marc, 'because we've got another question and it's nearly half past four.'

Loes pushed the box back under the settee, and Marjorie immediately lay down on the floor to look underneath it. She was singing something but the words weren't very clear because her cheek was pressed against the floor. So the song she was singing sounded very strange indeed. It sounded like ler, ler.

'What do you want to know?' asked Emil.

'Can you cook?' asked Marc.

'Yes, of course,' answered Emil.

'What?'

'All sorts of things.'

'Can you make mashed potato?'

'Of course,' said Emil.

'And can you cook roast beef?'

'That too.'

'And can you prepare peas and carrots?'

'I can do that as well.'

'And do you know how to cook chicory?'

'Yuk, chicory,' said Loes, and this set little Marjorie off again. She said yuk, yuk, yuk for quite a long time. After a while it began to sound like yer.

'And can you make chocolate pudding?'

'I can make chocolate pudding,' said Emil.

'And whipped cream?'

'And whipped cream,' said Emil. 'But why do you want to know?'

'They're all Monique's favourites,' said Marc. 'And what we'd really like you to do is prepare the supper before she comes home.'

Emil sat deep in thought for a moment. 'It feels like an examination,' he said after a while, 'and I'm not sure that I really like the idea. But if we're going to get that meal ready in time, then we'd better get a move on. And you'll have to help me.'

'O.K., O.K.!' shouted Loes and Marc.

Before very long the kitchen was a hive of activity: potatoes were being scrubbed in a twinkling, carrots were being scraped, the beef was sizzling in the cooker, pan lids were clattering.

'We mustn't let the chocolate pudding get cold,' said Emil, who had mixed cornflour, cocoa and sugar and was transforming the mixture with milk into a beautiful smooth dark brown custard.

Then something went wrong. Marc, who was whipping the cream, accidentally knocked his arm against the wooden spoon that was standing in the pudding. The spoon performed a somersault like a trapeze artist and then dived headlong, grazing Emil's grey jacket and drawing a sort of exclamation mark on his trousers before falling at last on to his shoes.

'Oh!' said Marc.

'It's nothing,' said Emil.

'How will you get it off?' asked Loes.

'Just pour the pudding into the bowls,' answered Emil. He scraped the pudding from his clothes with a knife but this didn't make them any cleaner. Dabbing with lukewarm water didn't help either; it left brownish patches that looked like a sort of map, uninhabited islands in a grey sea.

'Monique's bound to notice,' said Marc.

'Yes, she notices everything,' said Loes.

'Bah!' shouted Marjorie.

'Whenever she comes home and we've broken something or made a mess, she can tell right away,' said Loes.

'Do you remember that glass?' asked Marc. 'We hid a broken glass right at the bottom of the rubbish bin but she still knew that we'd broken something. She just seemed to know even though there was only a very small splinter left on the floor.'

'And do you remember the ornament that fell off

128

the cupboard when we were playing ball?' asked Loes. 'The head came off but we glued it back on. She still knew at once. She'd hardly come into the room when she said, "What's happened to that little bird?" She notices everything.'

'Once we looked in her dressing table to see if she'd bought Christmas presents for us. We found a parcel behind the handkerchiefs and on it was written in big letters: MIND YOUR OWN BUSINESS!'

'Have you got an apron by any chance?' asked Emil.

'That's a good idea,' said Loes. 'You'll be able to hide those dirty marks with an apron.'

Loes thought that the blue checked apron really suited Emil. She was amazed when he tossed the carrots in a pan with butter and sugar.

'It's called glazing,' said Emil.

He obviously enjoyed cooking, and nothing had gone wrong so far.


Then a key was inserted in the lock of the front door, and turned.

There was Monique. She put her bag in the corner and hung her coat on the hallstand. 'Hello,' she said. 'I'm home again.' And: 'What a nice smell in here! Are you cooking something?'

Marc kept her standing in the hall. 'Mum, you mustn't get cross.'

'Why not?' she asked. 'Have you made a mess? Or has something gone wrong? Though I must say it really does smell good.'

'No, the food's fine,' said Marc. 'We're having

roast beef, potato, chicory and chocolate pudding, but . . .'

'Have you broken something?'

'No, nothing like that,' said Marc. 'But we've got a visitor. Someone you weren't expecting. We've asked someone to eat with us.'

'A friend from school?' she asked.

'No, not exactly,' said Marc. 'Come into the kitchen. We don't know him either but he certainly knows how to cook!'

Monique couldn't have been more amazed when she walked into the kitchen and saw Emil standing at the cooker in her checked apron. And she was just as amazed when Loes led her to the table that had been laid with the best dinner service. Candles were burning and on the table was a vase of yellow flowers and a bottle of red wine.

'Sit down,' said Marc. 'Then I'll pour you a glass of wine and we'll explain everything.'

There was a strange atmosphere in the house. Hardly anyone said anything and every sound was ten times louder than usual, or so it seemed. Putting down a bowl sounded like a gunshot and moving a chair leg made a noise like an elephant. In a manner of speaking.

Every now and then someone did say something:

'How many serving spoons do we need?'

'Where are the napkins?'

'Shall I put the bowls on the table?'

But because everyone could hear themselves speak, they preferred to keep their mouths shut.

130

'Where do I sit?' asked Monique.

This was a difficult question and no one knew the answer.

Luckily Marjorie was there to break the silence. She said that she had blood in her arms and she tried to demonstrate this by pinching them. 'The blood's in there,' she chattered. 'Just look!'

On and on she went and then she spat out the piece of roast beef she had in her mouth.

Marc wished that the radio was on.

'Perhaps I'd better go,' said Emil. He had taken the chicory in cheese sauce out of the oven and put it on the table.

'Of course you mustn't,' said Monique. 'Sit down and eat with us. You've cooked it all so beautifully. I really want you to join us. But you do understand . . .'

After one or two glasses of wine something of a conversation began, and Emil said that if he'd known that the advertisement and the letter had been written by children, then of course he wouldn't have come.

'The letter was typed so neatly . . .' he said.

'Bah!' said Marjorie, as she finished her pudding.

And Emil told Monique how the pudding spoon had landed on his trousers.

'I'd already noticed that,' said Monique.

'Come on, let's do the washing up,' Marc said to Loes. And they did the washing up, cleared everything away and said hardly anything at all to each other.

'She was really surprised,' said Marc.

'Perhaps it won't work out,' said Loes.

131

'We can't watch the telly,' said Marc.

'We'll make some coffee for Monique and Emil, we'll put Marjorie to bed and then we'll go to sleep ourselves,' said Loes.

And when they were upstairs, Loes said to Marc: 'When I took in the coffee, they were sitting together on the settee . . .'

The following morning, Saturday the first of June, Marc and Loes were awake early as usual. They got the breakfast ready: coffee, tea, milk, sugar, rusks, two soft boiled eggs, two glasses of orange juice, some bread, cheese and jam. They carried it to Monique's bedroom.

Loes knocked and Monique called out: 'Come in!'

'Isn't Emil here any more?' asked Loes.

'What a strange pair of children you are,' said Monique as she sat up in bed. 'Of course he's gone. It could have been a very awkward situation . . .'

'It was nothing very special really,' said Marc. 'We only put in an advertisement asking for a father.'

'It's a very strange way of finding a father, if you ask me,' said Monique. 'And very dangerous too. And I really do think you've got a cheek, trying to find a friend for me.'

'Don't you want a friend then?' Loes asked.

'Well, maybe I do,' said Monique. 'But I certainly don't want you lot sticking your noses in.'

Marjorie came in with her bear that had no arms or legs. 'I want breakfast too,' she said.

She sat on the bed and helped herself to some breakfast.

132

'This is jolly good coffee,' said Monique. 'And a perfect egg, just soft enough.'

Marjorie wanted a spoonful of egg too and she gave a piece of bread to her bear.

'It's a good thing that you've woken me up so early,' said Monique. 'I've got to go out soon, as it happens.'

'Out where?' asked Loes. 'On Saturday?'

'I'm going to visit a friend.'

'Do we know this friend?' asked Marc. 'Does his first name begin with an E by any chance?'

'I'm not saying anything,' laughed Monique. 'Otherwise you'll start interfering again. I'll ask the lady next door to keep an eye on you because I won't be back till late.'

'We've nearly got a new father,' said Loes, 'so perhaps we'd better try and find a new mother now!'

'Colour of skin unimportant,' said Marc.

'You can forget that idea for a start!' Monique shouted.

'All we have to do is put in another advertisement!' laughed Marc.

It nearly turned into a pillow fight.